WAGS'

World

Playing the Game

By
Anonymous

PUFFIN

To all the footballers in my life. Keep on kicking.

PUFFIN BOOKS

Published by the Penguin Group
Penguin Books Ltd, 80 Strand, London WC2R ORL, England
Penguin Group (USA) Inc., 375 Hudson Street, New York, New York 10014, USA
Penguin Group (Canada), 90 Eglinton Avenue East, Suite 700, Toronto, Ontario, Canada M4P 2Y3
(a division of Pearson Penguin Canada Inc.)
Penguin Ireland, 25 St Stephen's Green, Dublin 2, Ireland (a division of Penguin Books Ltd)
Penguin Group (Australia), 250 Camberwell Road, Camberwell, Victoria 3124, Australia
(a division of Pearson Australia Group Pty Ltd)
Penguin Books India Pvt Ltd, 11 Community Centre, Panchsheel Park, New Delhi – 110 017, India
Penguin Group (NZ), 67 Apollo Drive, Rosedale, North Shore 0632, New Zealand
(a division of Pearson New Zealand Ltd)
Penguin Books (South Africa) (Pty) Ltd, 24 Sturdee Avenue, Rosebank,
Johannesburg 2196, South Africa

Penguin Books Ltd, Registered Offices: 80 Strand, London WC2R ORL, England

puffinbooks.com

First published 2009
2

The moral right of the author has been asserted
All rights reserved

Set in Sabon MT 10.5/15.5pt
Typeset by Palimpsest Book Production Limited, Grangemouth, Stirlingshire
Made and printed in England by Clays Ltd, St Ives plc

British Library Cataloguing in Publication Data
A CIP catalogue record for this book is available from the British Library

ISBN: 978-0-141-32580-4

www.greenpenguin.co.uk

Penguin Books is committed to a sustainable future
for our business, our readers and our planet.
The book in your hands is made from paper
certified by the Forest Stewardship Council.

1

For Amy Thornton, the party was almost perfect.

Chandeliers hung over luxurious furnishings in a room that was probably big enough to contain an entire football pitch. A staff of black-clad waitresses, all around Amy's age, smiled professionally as they swept by, offering silver trays of fancy nibbles. Huddles of glamorous, barely dressed girls laughed together and behaved every inch like they felt right at home in this glitzy mansion.

Amy was holding an elaborate-looking canapé on a stick and a fluted glass of champagne cocktail she'd been told was called a Meringue Royale.

It was all wonderful. But there was something missing.

Not something. Someone.

Damien.

Damien Taylor, rising star, who had made the move from Stanleydale United to the Royal Boroughs for a sum of money that got all the tabloids in a frenzy. Boy wonder, tipped for greatness, his name already pencilled in football's hall of fame.

Or rather: Damien Taylor, Amy's first and only boyfriend, the boy-literally-next-door from their West Yorkshire hometown. The boy who, two years ago, had stammeringly asked her out and then kissed her at the bowling alley. And they'd been totally, amazingly in love ever since. So much so that she'd saved up money from her weekend and holiday job and come all the way to London so they could spend the rest of summer side by side.

Except that he wasn't here.

Instead of Damien, she had Rosay ('*Like the wine*') standing next to her. Her new friend was scanning the room and explaining in gossipy detail exactly what was wrong with every victim her eyes landed on. Amy made polite noises in response. She'd only been in London a few hours and she wouldn't have felt right commenting on the dress sense and dating history of total strangers.

She didn't mean to, but she found herself tuning Rosay out and beginning a private game of 'spot the celebrity' instead, trying not to stare too much. It felt like some kind of dream, being surrounded by all these famous faces.

She gave herself three points for the actress and the girl-band member she spotted, and two each for the models, although she wasn't completely sure about those – most of the women here looked like models anyway. She only awarded herself one point for every footballer she recognized. It was a footballer's party, after all.

She'd already seen the party's host a couple of times, each time with his arm around a different woman, neither of whom were his girlfriend. But Damien wasn't the only absent team member, which could explain things. A few of them must have been asked to stay behind after the match.

Her sleb-spotting score was well into double figures when she heard Rosay say, 'Of course, everyone knows that there's no such thing as a faithful footballer, especially in the Premier League.'

Amy snapped out of her trance. 'I'm sure that isn't true.'

'It's very true. Not one, not ever. They're all the same.' Rosay's laugh was hollow. 'Sooner or later, they all cheat.'

Amy was sure that Rosay had been hurt in the past – she seemed to have an axe to grind, and she'd been chopping away all afternoon.

Rosay went on about temptation, boys being boys and footballers being anyone's. 'Seriously, Amy, you're lucky I'm here to warn you. Most of us find out the hard way.'

Amy brushed that comment aside. Damien wasn't that kind of guy. Her hand was immediately drawn to the delicate Tiffany necklace he'd given her when he moved to London. At the time, she'd joked that he should have bought something more practical instead. She could do with a new suitcase, for a start. But he'd said no; he wanted to get her something beautiful and long-lasting. But it wasn't the expensive heart-shaped pendant that made her sure of Damien; it was everything it stood for. Damien loved her. Damien was nothing like whoever had broken Rosay's heart.

Amy fiddled with the diamond cluster on the pendant. 'Look, I'm sorry. I've had a tiring day. I think I'll go back to the house,' she told Rosay, hoping it didn't sound too rude. After all, she'd been really lovely, going out of her way to help Amy adjust to this strange environment.

But she really should get back. Damien couldn't even contact her here. Rosay had insisted Amy leave her mobile behind because it would ruin the line of the tiny Miu Miu clutch bag she'd lent her. Even lip gloss and a key were testing its limits.

Anyway, surely after whatever had kept him, Damien would rush back to the house to see her. He was probably there right now, wondering where she was. He certainly wouldn't expect her to be all glammed up at some party he hadn't even mentioned to her.

But just then a rumble of deep voices filled the enormous space. Amy heard loud laughter accompanied by a chorus of 'One–nil!', 'Nice one!', 'Trounced 'em!' and various other celebratory calls as a group of men piled into the party.

It was the rest of the Royal Boroughs boys. They sounded a lot like Stanleydale's local team, but there was no doubt they looked different. Cleaner and smarter, for a start. And surrounded by girls who sparkled more brightly than the diamanté studs on Rosay's belt.

'You can't leave now,' Rosay declared. 'The rest of the boys have arrived!'

That's when, through the throng, Amy caught the words, 'Way-hey, the new boy's pulled at last! Fit bird, Taylor!' They were coming from a guy Amy thought she recognized as the Boroughs goalie, who had a leery smirk on his face. She followed his gaze.

And there he was at last. Damien – *her* Damien.

He was standing with a familiar-looking girl in a skimpy gold dress, and she was laughing as if he'd said something hilarious, and holding on to his arm.

Rosay gave Amy a worried look.

The gold-clad girl was none other than the chronic boyfriend-stealer Rosay had been warning her about all day.

2

Just a few hours earlier, when Amy had stepped through the arrivals gate and into her new life, she'd been too distracted by her phone to notice the commotion.

She'd smiled as she scrolled through at least five messages from Asha and one from Susila. Her twin best friends wanted to know if she was 'missing them already' (Susi), and whether she'd 'seen Coleen out shopping' or 'turned into VB yet' (typical Asha).

She tapped 'As if!' into her phone, followed by a row of kisses, and sent the same message to both of them. She was going to miss Susi and Asha, but she was glad they hadn't minded too much when she'd cancelled their plans for the summer. She and the twins always spent their break working at the local branch of Water World, chatting and laughing the second 'Big Ears', their annoying boss, had his back turned. But the twins knew that Amy was missing Damien big-time.

She'd been working as much as exams allowed anyway, saving up for ages to be able to afford time off, and she'd done a few weeks of full-time lifeguarding almost as soon as she'd put her pen down in her last GCSE. She'd saved up loads – easily enough to pay her way in London, especially since Damien told her accommodation was covered. He also insisted on paying for her travel. That's why she'd ended up travelling in luxury by plane when surely a cheapo coach trip would have got her there just as easily, if three times as slowly. She was definitely going to pay for everything else, though.

Even though Susi and Asha understood why Amy was going, they still teased her about being a footballer's girlfriend – officially a 'G' in 'WAG'. 'You'll never come back to this dump after all that glitz and glamour,' Asha had laughed. 'Besides, you'll want to keep a close eye on Damien now he's rich and famous!'

They'd agreed to keep her updated on West Yorkshire's finest gossip in exchange for stories about her amazing break – if that's all it was.

But Amy knew she was definitely coming home in September. She had plans, after all, and a life of her own. A long-distance relationship wasn't ideal, but she knew she and Damien would survive. They were rock solid.

Amy wrote a quick message to her mum and dad to say she'd arrived, everything was OK and she'd ring them later. She added extra hugs and kisses just before she hit 'Send'. After that, her pink phone displayed only a photo of a blonde girl and her athletic, dark-skinned boyfriend – Amy and Damien. A couple for so long that they were known as 'Amien' by friends, who claimed they were joined at the hip.

Amy smiled at the snapshot, put the phone in her pocket and looked up.

That was when she noticed the first flash.

'Amy, over here!'

'Amy! Smile!'

'Show us some attitude, love!'

She scanned the faces in front of her, looking for her boyfriend. They stared back, but none of them were Damien. Tall, muscular build? No. Warm brown eyes? Nope. Just scruffy jackets, gappy teeth and cameras, crowding towards her.

She tried to dart away from them, but her oversized, not-on-wheels suitcase slowed her down. Maybe she should have insisted that Damien buy her a suitcase instead of a necklace after all. Her parents' old battered monstrosity was perfect for family trips to Spain, but not so great for escaping unexpected paparazzi.

All around faces scowled at her, just like the flight attendant on the plane who had stopped her switching her phone on too soon. Amy blushed at the thought – she'd supposed you could get away with that sort of thing in business class.

'Can't be her, mate. Too rosy-cheeked!'

'And look at the outfit! Who wears *that* to go on an plane?'

'She's only sixteen, have a heart. Over here, love! Gizza smile!'

'Amy Thornton!'

'Mrs Damien Taylor!'

'Amy!'

It was overwhelming to hear so many odd-looking photographers call her name. Not that her name was 'Mrs Damien Taylor' anyway, although she had to admit she'd tried it out on paper a few times.

A man stepped through the throng. He was small with grey hair and wore a suit. He was different from the others – calmer, and without a camera.

'Miss Thornton?'

Amy nodded, although she hadn't been called that much either, or not since the time she'd skipped school for Damien's important football trial and she'd got into trouble with the head teacher.

The grey-haired man took her monster suitcase in one hand and marched away. She rushed after him and, before she knew it, she was outside the airport. A white limousine was parked there. Waiting for her. Wow. So this was what Damien's million-pound deal with the Boroughs was all about.

The throng of paparazzi were still surrounding her as the limousine door swung open.

'Amy!' *Flash!*

'Where did you buy your skirt? Or is it a belt?' *Snap!*

'Amy Thornton! Where's Damien?' *Flash! Snap!*

Amy covered her face with one arm. She hadn't expected this. Damien was the new star, not her.

Just before the limo door clunked shut, she was sure she heard one of the men laugh, 'They're going to eat her alive.'

The limo driver seemed like a nice man, but he either couldn't or wouldn't speak English.

'Where are you taking me?' Amy tried for the second time.

The man nodded and kept driving.

'Are you taking me to Damien? Damien Taylor? The footballer?'

The driver nodded slightly more vigorously.

'Is he at the Boroughs? Are you taking me to Stadium Gardens?'

The driver turned his head slightly and smiled at her.

Amy sighed, tugged her skirt down and leant back on the

leather seat. She stared out of the dark window, watching the wide grey suburban roads give way to the narrower, antique-looking lanes of west London. She'd seen this area on television – it was definitely close to where the Royal Boroughs played.

She wondered why she was being taken there. It was probably some kind of surprise Damien had planned for her. Maybe he wanted to show her around his new club. His new *Premiership* club – no more Stanleydale United Youth Team for him!

As the limo pulled up outside the unmistakeable seashell-like outline of Stadium Gardens, Amy felt her excitement rising. She hadn't spent this long away from Damien *ever*. She'd been at every one of his matches, cheering him on.

And he'd been there for Amy, too, encouraging her for the exams, and helping out on the worst days of her mum's illness and treatment. Amy's dad thought the world of Damien, and not just because he'd always wanted a son. He was all for letting Amy come to London, and he talked Amy's mum into it too. 'Hasn't this awful cancer scare taught us that life is for living?' he'd said. 'Our Amy should grasp every chance she can.'

And Amy certainly wanted the chance to be with Damien again, and gaze into his dark eyes and feel his fit arms around her. In fact, she didn't want to be without him a moment longer!

The driver held Amy's door open and she thanked him at least ten times.

Click! Flash! Whirr! She could do without all that, though. Amy shielded her eyes for the second time that morning as, again, a suited person appeared – a woman this time, dressed all in black – and whisked her away from the blinding lights.

Amy tried to strike up a conversation, but the woman just gave curt one-word replies as she led her through a gate and up some stairs.

What was it with everyone? Why would no one talk to her properly? Was it her northern accent – didn't they understand it in London?

The woman opened a door and led Amy into a room. Only it wasn't a room. The ceiling and walls were see-through. It was a box – a glass enclosure over the vast green of the football ground.

And it was filled with people. Not people – women. Girls, in groups. All sleek-haired and super-stylish. All staring at her. WAGs.

They were all dressed down by Saturday-night-in-Stanleydale standards – some were even wearing jeans. But they still all looked amazing.

Amy fought a strong urge to text Susi and Asha right away and describe the outfits being modelled in front of her.

'Um, hi,' she said instead, to the nearest faces.

A cool sea of eyes sized her up. No one spoke.

'I'm Amy.' Silence. 'Amy Thornton.' Silence. 'Damien Taylor is my boyfriend.'

That seemed to do the trick.

'Amy Thornton,' a voice near her drawled. 'You're the new *baby*.' The voice's owner was dripping with gold jewellery that contrasted perfectly with her smooth mocha skin and somehow seemed elegant rather than over-the-top, just like her classy-looking diamond-studded sunglasses. Amy thought she recognized them – both the shades and their owner. Yes

– Asha had drooled over sunglasses in last month's *Vogue*, and Amy had laughed because they cost about what her dad earned in a month at the council. And the owner – the owner was definitely Claudette Harris, married to Danny Harris, the Boroughs' long-established champion striker and fully fledged member of the England team. In all her years of browsing through Asha's magazines, Amy had never once seen a less than glamorous photo of Claudette Harris.

'Come over here, darling. Let's take a look at your baby-face.'

Amy felt herself flush with embarrassment. She wondered what would happen if she turned and ran out of the box. Would the paparazzi be waiting outside? Would that be better than this?

She stood still and swallowed hard. She had nothing to be ashamed of. 'I'm sixteen,' she said, stung at being described as a 'baby'.

'Aw, coochie-coo.' Claudette's jewellery jingled along with her laugh.

'God, Claudette, anyone would think you were ancient,' said a familiar and friendly looking girl with a smattering of freckles arranged prettily on her face. Amy realized with a start that she was looking at Paige Young, the singer of a summer hit she and the twins used to love.

Well, Amy knew that Claudette Harris wasn't all that old – she remembered reading about '18-year-old Claudette's secret island wedding' a couple of years ago. But faced with Claudette's real-life glamour right now, Amy felt like the age gap was way bigger than that.

'There's a world of difference between twenties and teens,'

Claudette drawled. 'As you know yourself, little Paige, barely out of nappies yourself.'

Paige shrugged pleasantly and pointed to an empty seat next to her. 'Don't listen to Claudette,' she said. 'She's just jealous of our youth. Come and sit here, Amy Thornton, and tell us all about the super-fit Damien Taylor.' She gave Amy a warm smile.

Amy was walking over when another girl grabbed her arm and mumbled something.

'Pardon?' Amy asked.

The girl gave her a meaningful look. She seemed different from the others – she had short, dark hair, for a start, but there was something else. Her clothes were gorgeous but slightly too tight and her make-up was caked on. Amy thought she understood. Maybe the dark-haired girl felt as out of place here as Amy did right now. Amy felt a rush of sympathy for her.

The girl spoke again. 'She's Paige Young. Used to be in that rubbish band called White Paige? She sang like sandpaper? That awful music-free racket called "Sweetheart"?'

Amy wanted to say that she knew who Paige Young was – after all, she'd seen her on enough magazine covers, and she'd danced to 'Sweetheart' loads of times – but the dark-haired girl didn't leave a long enough pause. She was now singing 'swe-eeetheart' in a silly, breathy voice.

Paige herself looked like she was trying not to laugh, but instead she said, 'Rosay, pur-*lease*.'

'Rosay?' Amy wondered out loud.

'Yeah, you know. Like the wine.' Paige giggled. 'Only spelt wrong.'

Rosay raised her voice and belted out, '*Swe-eeetheart, be mine! Swe-eeetheart, so fine!*'

Strange. Amy knew she'd be meeting Rosay Sands, who was the Boroughs manager's teenage step-daughter. Rosay and her mother lived with Italian 'Big Carl' himself, and the family had offered Damien a place to stay 'while he found his feet'.

But the Rosay she'd been expecting – the one she'd seen in so many magazines – had long blonde hair and a much fresher face. Amy wondered if this new look was a recent thing, and why the press hadn't gone on about it.

Rosay Sands stopped singing, misunderstanding Amy's confused expression. 'Well, I'm not surprised you've never heard of White Paige, Amy. They were one-hit wonders. Total trash. Anyway, Paige is way more famous for what she did to her bandmate, *among others*. Her main qualification is stealing boyfriends.'

'Oh, is that, like, an NVQ?' said a girl with huge blue eyes and an innocent expression. Everyone ignored her.

Amy remembered seeing Paige in the tabloids about a year ago, pictured leaving the courts behind a leggy woman with a black strip over her eyes. The 'mystery woman' had been accused of damaging thousands of pounds' worth of Paige's clothing in a 'revenge attack'. The black strip was pretty useless, as everyone guessed she was White Paige's backing singer Trina Santos, whose boyfriend Paige had just started seeing. But the scandal had blown over quickly when Trina was let off. The last Amy heard was that Trina was a successful model back in her native Brazil.

Paige wrinkled her dainty nose at the dark-haired girl. 'Oh, Rosay, *please*. I can't believe you'd bring that up.'

Rosay ignored her. 'Look, Amy, sit with me. I'll teach you who to watch out for. Like her, for a start.' She pointed a perfectly manicured nail at Paige. 'And most of the rest of them.'

Amy wasn't sure what to say.

'*Mi-aow*,' Rosay added in an exaggerated fashion. 'You know what I mean.'

'Oh,' said Amy.

'Why is Rosay pretending to be a cat?' the blue-eyed girl asked no one in particular.

Rosay narrowed her eyes. 'That's Kylie Kemp. She's thick.'

Kylie shrugged and smiled pleasantly.

Paige scowled at Rosay.

Claudette sighed. 'Give me strength! You're *all* babies.'

It certainly looked like Rosay was right about some of the girls being catty, anyway. Amy sat down next to her.

Rosay beamed triumphantly. 'So,' she said, 'what's it like dating Britain's hottest teenage millionaire? I bet you've got some stories.'

A whistle blew in the distance.

'Ssh!' said Paige. Her eyes were fixed intently on the pitch.

But Claudette looked straight at Amy and Rosay with an icy stare. 'The game's begun,' she said coolly.

3

Amy tried hard not to feel annoyed with Damien as she left the football ground.

This was partly because she knew she was being unfair. There was a lot of pressure on him now. It was understandable that he might forget to tell her he had a pre-season friendly on the day of her flight, a match where he was on the bench the whole time and she only caught one glimpse of him during the whole ninety minutes.

It was also perfectly possible that, when Damien remembered the match, he was unable to phone her to tell her. He'd known her mobile would be switched off for most of the morning, after all.

And, all credit to him, he had somehow managed to summon a limo to take her to the pitch. He'd also hired yet another suited person to bring her an envelope at the end of the game. The envelope contained keys, a scribbled address and a note saying, 'My place. The limo will take you to the main gates. Let yourself in and make yourself comfy. Damien xx'.

Yes, Amy decided, there was nothing to be annoyed about. Things were different now. Her football-mad boyfriend-next-door had become an eighteen-year-old

Premiership footballer. He lived in a mews cottage in the grounds of a mansion worth well over thirty-two million pounds, according to what Amy's dad had read in the *Daily World*. Some minor details of their fantastic relationship were bound to change.

Another reason Amy was trying to stay calm was that she had Rosay Sands with her – not that she wasn't grateful about that. Big Carl's step-daughter was the perfect person to help her navigate the various security gates and locks that led down the private road to Caseydene, a large white building decorated with pillars, black iron balconies and an ornate clock. By herself, Amy might have got lost in the grounds or stopped and gawped a lot more at the elaborately landscaped garden on the way to Damien's mews cottage.

The cottage looked small in the shadow of the impressive main building. Amy bit back a sudden urge to ask Rosay how many bedrooms they had – something her dad would definitely want to know later. She thought about the way Damien and his brother had grown up back in Stanleydale, sharing a small bedroom. The first thing little Stephen had said when he'd heard Damien's transfer news was, 'Great – I'll get the room to myself!' Amy couldn't imagine how it must feel to be Rosay and actually live here. The estate seemed far too big and grand for one family.

But Rosay completely ignored her surroundings and chattered on about the people Amy had just met and how nasty they all were.

Amy had felt sorry for Rosay earlier, but she was almost bursting with sympathy for her now, especially after what had happened at the end of the match.

Paige had mentioned 'the after-party at Scotty's place' and asked, 'You all coming later?'

'If I have nothing better to do,' Claudette had said, her eyebrows making a brief appearance over the top of her shades.

Rosay had cupped her hand over Amy's ear and whispered loudly, 'Scott White is Paige Young's boyfriend,' even though Amy knew that. Scott was the Boroughs' striker and part-time pop star – he couldn't sing but he'd raised White Paige's profile by appearing in their videos. He was the man that Paige had stolen from Trina Santos. He was famously good-looking and the most downloaded mobile-phone screensaver among Stanleydale's Year 11 girls.

'But you don't want to go to his place. It's thoroughly Essex.'

'Nah, you should come, Amy!' Paige had said, smiling. 'You can have your first taste of the Meringue Royale. It's heavenly.'

'The Meringue Royale is the official champagne cocktail for that lot – the Boroughs WAGs,' Rosay had told Amy. 'So super-tacky. I wouldn't go to that party if you paid me.'

Amy had never drunk any kind of cocktail, tacky or not. She and her friends sometimes drank cheap white wine at house parties in Stanleydale, and she'd had some champagne when Damien signed his contract.

'Paige wasn't inviting you, Rosay darling, let alone paying you,' Claudette had said. 'However badly you need the money.'

That was when Damien's envelope had arrived, right in the middle of Claudette's laughter at Rosay's expense. After Amy had read the contents twenty times and checked her blank phone again, Rosay had taken the note from her, sniffed and said, 'Let's go home.'

And here they were now, standing outside the mews cottage in the grounds of Rosay's huge house. Amy turned the key in the unfamiliar lock.

The door opened into a room that was wider than Amy's and Damien's family houses in Stanleydale put together.

'Unbelievable,' Amy breathed, taking in the marble floor and the minimalist furnishings. There was a white leather sofa at one end of the enormous room, opposite a plasma widescreen television. At the other end was a sparkling silver kitchen. Everything gleamed. Amy had never seen anything like it. The place was tardis-like and amazing.

'I'll say,' said Rosay, wrinkling her nose in disgust. 'It's tiny. Don't worry, sweetie, when Damien buys a place of his own you'll have plenty of space to spread out. And your own pool and gym. You'll have to share ours for now.'

She breezed past Amy, towards two closed doors beyond the kitchen. They were painted brilliant white and had yellow Post-it notes stuck to them.

Rosay peeled them off, giving Amy a curious glance. 'Awww, that's so sweet,' she said.

Amy went over to see what she was talking about. One note said 'Damien's room' and the other 'Amy's room'.

Amy felt her cheeks grow hot. 'That's Dad's fault,' she said, wondering why she felt the need to explain. On one hand, it was none of Rosay's business. On the other, Rosay might well have overheard the same excruciating conversation as Amy did, the one about the proposed sleeping arrangements for Amy's stay.

Amy's dad thought Carlo di Rossi was 'one of the most influential football managers in Britain'. This didn't stop him from asking the 'truly great man', his voice uneven with nerves and dignity, to 'keep an eye' on his daughter, 'because even though I trust her with my life, she is only sixteen, after all'. And she'd nearly died afterwards when her dad reported Carlo di Rossi's opinion that girlfriends were 'too distracting', but he'd just offered a work placement to a trainee sports psychologist who'd convinced him that personal relationships for players were important, according to research. Because of this, Amy would be 'welcome, with some conditions', one of which was separate bedrooms.

Amy was sure her face was glowing red now, just thinking about it.

'Well, you can do what you like now you're here, can't you?' Rosay laughed, sticking both the notes on the same door. 'Make Damien's day! I promise I won't tell Carlo.'

'Um, well . . .' Amy blushed even deeper. She barely even talked to the twins about that kind of thing.

Luckily, her new friend was wandering off towards the kitchen area and away from the subject of bedrooms altogether.

'More notes . . .? Oh!' Rosay scrunched some yellow paper in her hand, then stuck her head in a fridge that, by herself, Amy would have taken ages to find, because the door was disguised as part of the wall.

'What do they say? "Damien's kitchen"? "Amy's fridge"?' Amy tried to joke, but Rosay seemed distracted.

'Mm, yeah, that's right,' she said. 'The fridge is almost empty. Needs a woman's touch.'

Amy laughed because she wasn't exactly the kind of woman Rosay was talking about. Amy loved shopping for clothes with her mates, but faced with supermarket produce, she drew a complete blank. When her mother was laid up, her dad had taken over all the food side of things, and Damien had occasionally helped. He was a pretty good cook – his speciality was spicy jerk chicken, thanks to his mum.

Rosay wasn't joking. 'It's good that you're here now to take care of him. Footballers need special diets, you know, for strength.'

'Oh, right,' Amy said.

'Didn't you know that?'

'Yeah, kind of.' She also knew Damien's favourite meal was chips with curry sauce. She didn't see any harm in that, not with the amount of running about he did. There was no way he was remotely unhealthy.

Rosay tutted. 'Amy, you *can* cook, can't you?'

'Er, not really.'

Rosay sighed. 'I'll have a word with Mum. She was supposed to be overseeing this side of things, but she's obviously been too busy redecorating and party planning to notice, as usual.'

Rosay pressed a button and a separate section of the fridge sprang open. She took out a gold-labelled champagne bottle and began to untwist the wires securing the cork. Amy wondered what it was doing in Damien's fridge. Her boyfriend was generally more the lager type when it came to parties, and he'd all but given up since he'd signed the deal with the Boroughs.

Rosay selected two fluted crystal glasses from another hidden unit. Then she opened a few more drawers and cupboards and pulled out swizzle sticks, pre-cut slices of lime and a box of fruit juice. She certainly seemed to know where everything was in here and, apart from the fruit juice, they were all things Amy would never have expected to see in Damien's house.

Of course, it was Carlo di Rossi's house, not really Damien's, which explained it. When Damien had first moved in and she'd asked him what it was like, he'd said, 'Weird, Ames. Not exactly home, you know. But don't worry, I'm fine and it's just for a while. And I'll be made up if you can come down for the summer!'

Amy watched Rosay line up the ingredients on the counter. 'So who normally lives in the mews cottage?' Amy asked. 'I mean, who was here before Damien?'

'No one, not since . . . Well, Carlo thought Damien should stay in the guest annexe but then Mum decided to completely redecorate it and it still isn't finished, so Damien had to come here.' Rosay shrugged. 'Want some fizz? I'm sure Damien won't mind if we celebrate your arrival together.'

'Er, no. No thanks.' Rosay was starting to unnerve her. Amy longed to ring Susi and Asha and have a normal girlie chat about her day so far. Preferably right after she phoned Damien and found out why he wasn't here and when she'd see him. And then she'd ring her mum and describe every last detail of this gorgeous house.

But not with an audience.

Amy looked around, wondering how to say it. 'You know, Rosay, I should really . . .' She noticed her monster suitcase neatly tucked in a corner, by the sofa. The limo driver must have brought it in earlier. 'I need to unpack now.'

'I'll help you,' Rosay said. She poured herself a small glass of champagne, added a splash of juice and a piece of lime.

Then she threw a swizzle stick in with an expert flourish and took a sip before clicking her heels over to the sofa and sitting down in a flash of Christian Louboutin red soles.

Amy unlocked her suitcase and tried not to sigh as Rosay got up, heaved it on to its side and started pulling out Amy's clothes, scanning labels and making remarks the whole time. 'What possessed you to buy that one? George? Atmosphere? Papaya? Who *are* these designers? Omigod, I've never seen anything like that. It's not just your boyfriend who needs extra care and attention! I know some of the other girls can get away with a high-street look if they mix it with designer, but you're not in that league yet, Amy.'

Amy's best clothes were all over the floor. She picked up a strappy green dress, one of her favourites, and stroked it lightly. It had been a bargain in the sale at Harvey Nics – a real find. She'd nearly had a fight with Asha over who saw it first.

Rosay shook her head. 'And don't even think about wearing last season's ready-to-wear Chloé. Honestly. They'll laugh at you. Even our concessions to the high street have to be seasonal and sold out before they officially hit the rails.'

Amy felt suddenly rebellious. After all, she didn't need those girls' approval, just because her boyfriend was on the same team as theirs. She loved that dress. 'Maybe I don't care.'

Rosay gave her a sharp look. 'Of course you care. Or you may as well go back to Smalltown right now.'

'I'm from Stanleydale.'

'Yes, exactly. Listen. As long as you're still with Damien Taylor, you're involved with those vultures whether you like it or not. You have to learn to play the game, Amy. If you don't, Paige will steal Damien from under your nose. And watch out for Claudette, too. She acts like she's better than everyone, and she stabs people in the back – be ultra careful what you tell her. Kylie's stupid, so you don't have to worry about her, just keep out of her way. Trina's gone for now, a relief for nearly everyone. And the others ... Amy, are you listening? You do agree, don't you?'

Amy put her dress down. 'Agree with what?'

'With what I said. About the girls.'

Amy realized her mind had been wandering. 'Yes, I suppose so. They did seem kind of ... catty, like you said.'

'Trust me, they are. Anyway, if you stick with me, you should be OK. Did you notice that they're all scared of me? I can cause trouble for them and their boyfriends, you know, just like that!' She clicked her fingers. 'And talking of boyfriends, where is Damien, anyway? Shouldn't he be here with you by now?'

Amy bit her lip. She'd been thinking the same thing.

Rosay was watching her closely. 'Oh, Amy. Are you having second thoughts about all this? I don't blame you – it's a lot of pressure having a boyfriend in the Premiership. I'm here to help you. Come on, tell me all about it.' She got up and walked over to the kitchen to pour herself another small flute of champagne.

So Amy had a bit of a moan about Damien, and she had to admit it felt good to let her irritation out. Why had he still not called her? Typical lad!

'And he didn't even leave you a note explaining where he'd be,' Rosay sighed, glancing towards the fridge. 'Or plan anything special for your first night back together. Oh, Amy, you poor thing.'

Rosay put down her empty glass and picked up one of Amy's newer purchases, a backless Warehouse dress that Amy had never felt entirely comfortable in. 'I'll tell you what to do. You put this on and touch up your make-up. I'll take you to Scott White's party, and you show Damien you can cope just fine without him.'

Amy was startled. She didn't want to make any kind of statement like that. She just wanted to find Damien and hear his explanation, because he was sure to have one, and then she wanted to fall into his arms and start their dream summer together. 'But I thought you didn't want to go to the party?'

Rosay sighed. 'I'd go for you, Amy – for a friend,' she said. She picked up Amy's favourite green dress. 'I'll do you a favour and take this off your hands. It'll be quite loose, but I'll belt it. Come on, let's show them all.'

4

Amy's heart sank as all her plans for a happy reunion with Damien flew out of the diamond-paned, leaded windows of Scott White's penthouse apartment.

For a start, she was annoyed with the goalie for saying Damien had 'pulled a fit bird'. She could imagine what Susi and Asha would say about that – back home she and the twins *never* let boys get away with remarks like that!

Secondly, Damien definitely had some explaining to do, turning up at the party with a glittery girl on his arm, when as far as he knew she was waiting for him back at the flat like Stanleydale's answer to Cinderella. She hadn't even had a note from him since the one that arrived with the keys!

But despite the laddish remarks, and everything Rosay had been saying about disloyal footballers, she didn't really think there could be anything going on between Damien and Paige Young. Paige was holding on to Damien's arm, for a start, not the other way round.

And Damien didn't look very comfortable with it, even before he noticed Amy when his face lit up.

Amy loved the way he got twitchy around other girls – she

always teased him about it. 'You *are* allowed to have female friends, you know,' she'd joke. And he'd reply something like, 'But girls never want to be friends with me. They all fancy me like crazy!' Then he'd laugh and sweep her into his arms, and kiss her and say, 'But I don't care because you're the only one for me.'

She was so happy to see him but she was so angry he was here!

He looked like he was about to say something to her, but suddenly Rosay was standing between them with her hands on her hips. Her face managed to look red even through the mass of foundation Amy had watched her put on earlier.

'You just can't resist other people's boyfriends, can you, Paige?'

A lad behind Damien said, 'Ooh, catfight!'

It was the Boroughs goalie again, with the same excited smirk.

But Paige laughed. She said pleasantly, 'Oh, Rosay, *please* get over it, would you? I've let it go, why can't *you*? Anyway, I'm sure Amy can speak for herself.'

Amy nodded, though she couldn't really think of a single thing to say, and actually it *was* starting to bug her a little that Paige still had her arm looped around Damien's.

The goalie slunk away, looking disappointed that there wasn't going to be an argument after all.

Paige smiled at Amy. 'Amy, I had to physically drag Damien here to look for you. He was moping about at *Les Jardins* like a lost soul.' She finally moved her arm, looking pointedly at Rosay. 'I'm off to find Scotty. You should leave the lovebirds to it, Rosay.'

'I'm staying right here – *my friend* needs me,' Rosay said to Paige's retreating back.

Amy wasn't sure if that was true but she still didn't say anything. What exactly had just happened? What was Paige talking about – Damien was *where* like a *what*?

On top of all the uncertainty, she felt . . . well, weird. After more than a month away from her, Damien was finally within hugging distance. He looked the same – gorgeous body, tufty dark hair, deep brown eyes – but his clothes were different. Smarter. She'd never seen him wear trousers like those before – they weren't part of his sports kit, that was for sure.

She was hit by a sudden shyness. What was going on? She'd never felt like this around Damien before, not even on their first date. Damien had been ultra-quiet, which he later admitted was because he liked her so much he couldn't think straight. She'd felt the same way about him, but in a comfortable, happy way. Being with him was like being at home – it always had been. It felt right.

But right now she was miles from home, irritated that he was at the party, thrilled to see him and totally nervous, all at the same time. She couldn't think of a single way to express any of that.

He seemed pretty tongue-tied, too, but he gave her that sexy smile that almost made her forget everything.

'Ames,' he said. 'Brilliant! You're here! I've been trying to call you for over an hour!'

'I left my phone at the cottage.' So he *had* tried to call. It really was all just a misunderstanding, as she'd suspected.

She longed to wrap her arms around him, but Rosay pulled her aside and whispered loudly, '*Les Jardins* is a cosy twosome sort of restaurant, you know. Ask him what he was doing there with *Paige*!'

Damien took a step closer. 'What are you talking about, Rosay?'

He looked genuinely confused, Amy had to give him that. And nothing about this quite made sense.

'Amy, didn't you get my note?'

Rosay muttered, seemingly to herself, 'That's right. Cover your guilt with notes.'

Damien frowned. 'Can we talk somewhere else, Ames?'

'Er . . .' said Amy.

'Fine,' Rosay said calmly. 'Of course. I understand.' She pointed to a tray of Meringue Royales resting on a mahogany table in the distance. 'I'll be over there if you need me.'

With Rosay gone, Amy found her voice at last. 'Damien, you could have called earlier! If it wasn't for Rosay, I'd still be sitting on my own at the cottage! While you're busy out and about who-knows-where!'

'But I was waiting for you at the restaurant.' Damien's voice went very quiet. 'It was supposed to be kind of . . .' He took another step towards her and mumbled, 'Romantic, or something. Like the notes.'

'The last note I got from you was the one with the keys!'

'Really? Oh no! There were two more.' His frown deepened. 'I really wanted tonight to be special. I've missed you.'

Amy felt her insides melt. 'I've missed you too.'

Damien put his arm around her and Amy couldn't help herself. She drew him closer and kissed him.

It was even better than she remembered. All the day's worries left her and she felt OK. Better than OK. Amazing.

She was with the best-looking, most wonderful person in the room, and she felt like a million dollars.

But a couple of seconds into the kiss, she felt suddenly conscious of all the glamorous celebrity types around her. They probably didn't go in for public displays of affection. Maybe she looked like some kind of kid at a school disco. She was showing herself up. And Damien, too.

She stopped kissing Damien and laughed nervously. 'Now everyone will *really* think you've pulled.'

'Ames, the lads have been ribbing me non-stop about you since I arrived in May! That's what they meant before when they said I'd pulled – they *recognized* you!' He gave her a gorgeously shy smile. 'I might have mentioned you once or twice, plus they all remember that lifeguard picture of you from the Sunday papers.'

Amy felt herself blush. Until today, that had been her only experience with the paparazzi – the time they'd snapped her at Water World, just after Damien's transfer deal went through. At least at the airport today she'd been wearing more than a swimsuit.

'But don't worry, they're not disrespecting you.' He put his fists up in mock-fight mode. 'They know they'd have me to answer to.'

'Ooh, yeah, I bet they're really scared,' she joked. Damien was notoriously fair and level-headed – the kind of guy that broke up fights and got everyone wondering what they'd disagreed about in the first place.

He laughed, hugged her close and kissed her again, but she pulled away, still feeling weird and nervous. She glanced around, but no one was watching them.

Amy sighed. What was wrong with her? Maybe everything Rosay had told her this afternoon about the other girls was having an effect on her.

Damien took her hand. 'Come on, you've got to see the roof terrace. I've been dying to show you – the way these people live is incredible. Guess how many cars Scott has?'

'I don't know. Three?'

'Five! And two are Hummers. Amazing or what?'

'Amazing,' Amy agreed. 'Wow, but Day, you could probably buy a car now too, if you wanted to.' Sometimes it shocked her when she thought about the amount of money Damien earned. She considered her lifeguarding a skilled job, but she got pretty much minimum wage for it, even though it was set to go up when she turned seventeen in the autumn. 'You could probably buy *five* cars.'

Damien shrugged as he led her up an ornate staircase and on to a large garden terrace with a view over the rooftops of west London and, in the distance, the muddy streak of the Thames. 'I keep offering to buy a car for Mum, but she insists she loves that battered Peugeot. In some ways, though, I know what she means. And why would anyone need more than one car? Or all these things.' He gestured around at the expensive-looking statuettes, marble bench and elaborate water feature. He glanced down. 'You only have one pair of feet, so you only need one pair of shoes, don't you? Well, and a couple of pairs of football boots, of course.'

'Oh God, no!' Amy laughed. 'You need a lot more than one pair of shoes!' She perched lightly on the edge of the marble bench and admired her latest favourites – two-tone Chloé-esque wedges from H&M. She and Damien often teased each other about shopping – Damien just didn't understand Amy's fascination with updating her wardrobe and trying out new styles. When Damien wasn't wearing his sports kit, he was strictly a plain-jeans-and-T-shirt kind of guy.

Except tonight, of course.

Damien came over and sat next to her, putting his arm around her in the warm glow of the sunset.

'Hey, when did you get those new trousers? They look designer.'

Damien brushed his free hand on them. 'Er, yeah, they're some Italian make.'

'Some Italian make?' She looked closer. 'Aren't they from that new Danny Harris range, with Armani? You're wearing Armani trousers!' She gave a loud laugh. 'OK, what have you done with the real Damien Taylor?'

The sheepish look on his face made Amy want to kiss him again.

'Anyway, they suit you. You look great,' she told him. Then she had another thought. 'You know, I still don't understand about tonight. How was I supposed to find you in this restaurant? Even if you'd told me in a note, I never would have found the place. I haven't got a clue where I am right now!'

'Oh, I left you a phone number for a car to take you there. And a couple of notes leading to the number – like a trail. I spent ages on it all.' Damien frowned. 'I can't believe you didn't get them! The cleaner must have moved them.'

'Wow, you have a cleaner?'

'Yes, every day! And a laundry service. Mum's going spare – you know how proud she is of the way she's trained me

31

and Stephen. She says she'll never speak to me again if I forget how to pick up my own socks.'

Amy laughed. She could just imagine Damien's bossy but lovely mother shouting those exact words, and meaning them, too.

'Anyway, *we* have a cleaner. You're here! It's ace.' He smiled and fiddled with Amy's heart pendant.

'Yeah.' She touched his arm. 'So why couldn't I see you sooner? Where were you after the match?'

'I knew I'd have to stay behind – Big Carl does these mega talks for the newest team members. Seriously, they go on for hours. Paige said you'd probably want to change and stuff, so I arranged to have your case dropped at the house and sent you the note with the keys. I had to get ready at the ground. This morning, Paige reminded me to take my smart clothes so I could go straight to the restaurant.'

Amy bristled at the mention of Paige, then told herself to calm down. 'And it was some French place?' When she and Damien went out for meals, it was usually to TGI Friday's in Leeds.

'Yeah, Paige recommended *Les Jardins* – she said . . .'

He'd said Scott White's girlfriend's name three times now, not that Amy was counting.

'Paige seems to have been very involved in all this.'

Damien pulled away a bit and looked at her. 'I s'pose she was.' He traced a pattern in the marble with his finger. 'I wanted to get . . . You know. A girl's view. I'm rubbish at that stuff. I wanted tonight to be perfect.'

Amy didn't think he was rubbish at that stuff at all, and now her stomach was starting to hurt. 'So you asked Paige?'

'Well, yeah. Scott's been a real mate since I got here. He's a good person. I see him and Paige a lot.'

'And she reminded you about your clothes?' Amy felt she had to add, 'This *morning*?'

'Well, yeah, she did. When she was about to drive me – and Scott – to Stadium Gardens.' Damien rubbed both hands on his trousers as if he was nervous.

'Oh, right. And did Paige help you pick out the Danny Harris clothes, too?' She hadn't meant to sound so *accusing*, but . . . well, actually, maybe she had.

'Yeah.' Damien folded his arms. 'Look, Paige is a friend. Is that a problem?'

Amy folded her arms, too. She wasn't sure of the answer.

Damien shook his head. 'Come on, don't be like this, Ames. You know how much I've been looking forward to seeing you. You've read all the texts I've sent –'

'You didn't send any today.'

'I thought you'd like the notes instead. I thought they'd be more, I dunno, personal, or something.'

'Oh, did *Paige* say that?'

His eyes blazed then. 'Will you listen to yourself! What's the *matter* with you?'

'Keep your voice down. What's the matter with *you*?'

They glared at each other. Amy's heart was pounding. What if Rosay was right? What if Paige Young, notorious boyfriend stealer, was just waiting for the right moment to pounce on her Damien?

And – worse – what if he wanted her to? Maybe he was even encouraging it – spending time with Paige, choosing clothes with her!

33

But Paige was with Scott White, wasn't she? Amy knew she was overreacting.

She needed to get Susi or Asha's opinion on this, and fast. If only she hadn't left her phone at home. If only Damien wasn't sitting right next to her, looking angry. And hurt.

A tendril of Amy's fancy up-do, courtesy of Rosay, fell into her face. Even her hair had given up.

Then Damien sighed, reached over and pushed the strand behind Amy's ear. 'Ames. Can we start this whole conversation again?'

When she nodded, her head felt heavy. It had been a long day.

'What's up with you really? It can't be about Paige. You're always saying I should be more matey with girls.'

She shrugged.

'You made me go shopping with Asha that Saturday before I left!'

Amy gave a small smile. 'Susi had flu, Dad needed me at home, Asha needed a skirt for work and she can't stand shopping on her own,' she remembered. 'But she said you were useless.'

'Exactly! I haven't got a clue about shopping! Or girls' stuff. And I wanted to make up for not meeting you off the plane. So I asked my mate's girlfriend for advice. That's all.'

Amy sighed. 'OK.'

'OK? *OK?* You put me through all that and then you just say "OK"?' He looked furious, but there was a glint in his eye. 'Come here,' he said. He kissed her till she was dizzy and then said, 'There. *Now* it's OK.'

She had to agree.

'Well, I'm glad that's sorted.' He stretched his arms out like a contented cat. 'So what do you think of the cottage? Isn't it massive? Have you seen the swimming pool? Have you met Mrs Carlo di Rossi yet?'

'No.'

Damien smiled. 'You're in for a treat. She's like a Rottweiler crossed with a poodle crossed with a loudspeaker. She makes my mum look shy and retiring.'

'Can't wait.' Amy shifted closer to Damien as they chatted, catching up on all the details of their weeks apart that they hadn't been able to cram into phone calls and text messages. He was the most wonderful guy in the world, without a doubt, and just as gorgeous as she remembered.

So why did this small, niggling part of her still feel uneasy about Paige Young?

5

'Babe, believe me, you do *not even* want to go there! Oh, no, no, no!'

The raucous voice cackled behind the side entrance to the main house, so loud that it made Amy's ears ring even though she was standing outside and she was sure the walls of Caseydene were pretty thick.

Damien nudged Amy. 'So what do you reckon, Ames? Do *you* even want to go there?' His eyes sparkled.

'Sunday lunch with Barbie, after everything you've told me? No, I don't. I want to turn and run all the way back to Stanleydale,' she said, only partly joking.

'Well, tough.' He laughed. 'This is your fault! I've been politely refusing Rosay's offers of brunch, dinner, Chihuahua tea and every other meal in the world from the minute I got here, but apparently *someone* arrived yesterday and convinced her I don't eat properly, and now she's got her whole family involved.'

'I bet it was Chai tea, Damien.' She sniffed. 'And I didn't mean to suggest you couldn't look after yourself. I know you can.'

'Yeah, but it's too late now. I can't exactly say no to Big Carl, can I? Even on my day off.'

Damien was smiling, but she wouldn't have blamed him if he'd been annoyed with her. Apparently, as a result of Amy's conversation with Rosay yesterday, Damien had been summoned to the house for Sunday lunch, and Big Carl would get someone to oversee Damien's food supply from now on. 'I want my players on top form! I don't hire the dietician for nothing!' they'd heard Carlo boom in the courtyard earlier, seconds before Rosay knocked at their door to tell them the news.

It was eleven in the morning by then, and Amy and Damien had been cuddling on the sofa, watching some soapy omnibus and enjoying what Damien said was a rare day off for him.

'That girl is a pain, Ames, I don't care what you say,' Damien said after Rosay left.

'Well, she was dead friendly yesterday, honestly,' Amy insisted. 'She just got a bit over-protective, that's all. I think she's been hurt by some footballer and she's trying to stop the same thing happening to me.'

'As if I'd ever hurt you!' Damien pounced on her and tickled her until she screamed for mercy. When they got their breath back, he said, 'Well, OK, but I still think she deliberately tried to ruin our night.'

Damien had found the missing notes last night when they'd got back from the party. The Post-its were all scrunched up on the counter together with some foil from the champagne. But Amy told Damien that Rosay must have peeled them off and thrown them aside without reading them and realizing how important they were.

Damien wasn't convinced and they'd nearly had a row about it, but Amy had managed to prevent it, saying they were both tired and they should talk about it in the morning.

Which was now.

She tried to keep her voice neutral. 'You weren't here, Day. To be honest, I think Rosay was a bit fed up and just fancied a quick drink.'

'Yeah, and that's another thing.' He pouted, looking a lot like his little brother. 'That champagne was supposed to be for you. It was supposed to be special!'

Then the only way Amy could stop herself from making a remark about *Paige* liking champagne, and dredging up *that* argument, was to cuddle up to Damien and change the subject completely. They made plans for their day together. Damien wanted to show her the sights of London, which he hadn't really had time to see himself yet.

'I wanted to wait and go with you, anyway,' he said, pulling her close and kissing her.

But before they could indulge in their dream afternoon together, Amy and Damien had to have lunch at the big house. It was a scary prospect. Barbie di Rossi seemed even worse than Damien had warned she'd be. She was the loudest woman in the world.

Amy and Damien heard her again, her voice carrying through the wall like a foghorn. 'So I said to him, babe, I said, babe, should I get another boob job? The left one's never been quite right!'

They caught each other's eyes and tried not to laugh.

Damien straightened his face first. 'Come on, we don't want to be late. We'd better knock.'

'You do it.'

'Why? You scared?'

'Yes.'

Damien laughed and reached for the brass football-shaped knocker.

But before he could use it, the door opened and there stood Carlo di Rossi himself.

He looked even bigger than he did on television, and more groomed. His head of grey-streaked hair was carefully styled and his Hugo Boss suit and tie were neatly pressed. The papers often made fun of Big Carl for spending more time on his appearance than he did on football, but Amy knew that couldn't be true. Damien said the Royal Boroughs had gone from strength to strength since Big Carl's arrival two years ago, and they certainly seemed to keep winning those cups. He also had a reputation for expecting a lot from his players, but giving them no-holds-barred support and enthusiasm in return. It was one reason Damien had been over the moon when the offer came in, even though it meant moving to London. 'He's only the *best*, Ames!'

Big Carl was displaying that enthusiasm right now. 'Ah! Damien Taylor!' he declared, slapping him sharply on both shoulders at the same time in an almost-hug. 'My newest great hope!'

Amy giggled and Damien shot her a silencing look.

'A young man with so much promise! Oh. You must be the little Amy.' He let Damien go and stopped smiling, although he did kiss Amy, once on each cheek. 'I told your father I'd keep an eye on you and I intend to do just that. But I hope you do not distract Damien from his important work.'

Amy didn't know what to say to that, but Big Carl didn't seem to expect a reply. 'So. It gives me pleasure that you're here for lunch.'

'Uh, yeah. Rosay told us to come,' Amy mumbled.

'Yes, yes, I told her to do this. You must come in.' He put his hands together as if he was about to pray. 'I am so sorry I cannot stay, but I have urgent business to attend to. There is no day of rest in football. And, Damien, our cook has special instructions for you. You must eat for strength. I'm expecting you at training later this afternoon.'

Amy looked at Damien in alarm. But it was his day off! They had plans!

'Er . . . oh,' Damien said. 'Today?'

'It's an extra session, it's true. I will be calling the other boys and expecting you all at three o'clock. I can't have a repeat of yesterday. It's less than two weeks till the start of the season!'

'But they won yesterday!' Amy blurted. She avoided Damien's eyes because she knew he'd be shocked at her bold-ness. But she couldn't help it! She'd been really looking forward to their afternoon together.

'The performance was poor. One goal, against a defence like that? Poor! We must fix it before the season starts. The team is not . . .' he gestured with his palms, pushing them together and meshing his fingers, 'properly gelled. They play like individuals! Is no good!' The manager shook his head vigorously, sounding more Italian the more heated he got. His grey curls didn't move an inch. His team might not be prop-erly gelled, but his hair certainly was.

'I will see you later, Taylor!' Big Carl slapped Damien on the back. 'Go in, go in. My girls will take care of you. And Josh is here, too.'

They obeyed, and found themselves in an ornate hallway

surrounded by trophies, certificates and framed team photographs. The walls were dark brown and the place felt like some kind of museum: a shrine to football.

'Who's Josh?' Amy asked Damien. What she really wanted to ask was, 'Can't you skip the training?' but she thought she'd start small.

'He's a sports psychology student who's on some kind of work placement. Big Carl says every good team has a psychologist these days, and this guy is the son of one of his oldest friends, an expert who works with a famous rugby team. I think Big Carl's doing his mate a favour and trying out this psychology thing at the same time.'

Amy giggled again. 'A psychologist? What's he going to do – ask you how you feel about kicking a ball?'

But Damien didn't smile. 'Ames, this is my big break – you know that. I want to make a go of it.'

'Course you do. I'm only joking.' She took his hand and he squeezed it, but she felt it again, that uneasiness from the night before, like something was different between them. She decided not to mention the extra training.

'Ah, here you are!' The foghorn voice was right in the room with them. 'Would you look at you two?' The voice's owner stood before them, petite and yet somehow larger than life, her blonde hair piled high on her head and her curves squeezed into a tiny Gucci sundress. 'Love's young dream! You're total pin-ups, the pair of you! That skin! Oh, to be young again!' She patted her bum with both hands. 'Course I can be, thanks to my surgeon!'

She gave that raucous laugh they'd heard through the walls.

'Hiya, Barbie,' said Damien. 'All right?'

'I am now that you're here, gorgeous!' Barbie laughed.

Amy cringed. Poor Rosay – imagine having a mother like this! No wonder she seemed to have problems.

Suddenly Barbie leant over her and cupped Amy's chin with one hand, pinching lightly. Amy grimaced. 'So you're the sweetheart we've been hearing all about? Well, you're sweet all right, babe, but my Rosay's right, you need the fashion police, and fast!'

Amy was shocked. She might not be in a Gucci dress, but she'd put quite a lot of thought into her outfit. It had to be appropriate for a morning of lounging on the sofa with Damien and an afternoon of sightseeing. For lunch she'd thrown some glamorous-looking Zara accessories at her practical outfit. She was wearing a summery dress from Topshop and the super-comfy Ugg boots Damien had bought her for Christmas. Asha said the large earrings gave her a wild but glam look.

'Never mind, babe,' Barbie said. 'I've got the best idea. Rosay!'

There was a silence.

'Rosay!'

Amy was sure the stone walls shook.

Rosay appeared in the doorway, looking fed up. 'What, Mum? Oh, hi, Amy.' She hesitated. 'And Damien.'

Rosay had changed her clothes since she'd come round to see Amy and Damien this morning, and for some reason Amy found she couldn't take her eyes off what she was wearing. There was something about it. The gypsy top was nice – maybe not the latest fashion, and again less dressy than Amy would have expected from someone like Rosay, but it had a certain style to it. But the green mini-skirt she was wearing with it was very familiar. Too familiar.

It was Amy's favourite Chloé dress!

Half of it! It had been butchered!

Amy shook her head. She had to be imagining things. Rosay had to own a mini skirt that precise shade of green, in that exact material.

'I'm gonna ring Orange County, honey,' Barbie was telling Rosay. 'I'm arranging a private shop for you and Amy for this afternoon. How does that sound?'

'Does that mean I can have the –' Rosay glanced at Amy, then at the door. 'You know. Can I talk to you in private a minute?'

Outside, Barbie lowered her voice so that the walls probably breathed a sigh of relief, but Amy could still hear her. 'No, Rosay. Rules is rules, you know that. You just help your new friend, OK?'

'You're so mean.' Rosay's voice carried. 'You're ruining my life!'

'Babe!' Barbie sounded hurt.

Rosay walked back into the room, smiling at Amy as if she hadn't been shouting a minute before. 'I'm looking forward to shopping with you, Amy. It's going to be so much fun.'

6

Lunch with Barbie and Rosay was only slightly less crazy than everything that happened before it. They sat round a massive oblong table covered in a silky cloth with rose petals sprinkled all over it. Barbie shouted happily at everyone and picked at a lettuce leaf, while Rosay didn't even glance at her salad.

Josh the psychology student had apparently been invited because he was new in town and didn't know anybody yet. Barbie went on about how Big Carl had talked to his course tutors. 'I heard you was the brainiest in that college of yours! And you've already passed some exams in counselling or something? Carlo's always on about what a good bloke your dad is, too, and an expert sports shrink and all. You probably don't even need all that study, eh? It's in your blood!'

Josh smiled pleasantly. He was tall and athletic and looked about the same age as Damien, though Amy thought he must be a year or two older because he talked about starting at university in the Midlands and how he missed the rugby 'back home'.

'Oh, are you from Australia?' she asked, because she thought she recognized his accent.

Barbie's laugh sounded like a demented chicken. 'He's going to kill you for that!'

Amy felt herself blush. Had she said the wrong thing?

'No, it's OK,' Josh said with a kind smile. 'I get that a lot, over here. I'm from New Zealand, though I've been in England for nearly two years now.'

'He's a Kiwi!' Barbie shrieked, though Amy couldn't really see what was so funny about that. 'No disrespect, Josh babe!'

But Josh kept smiling calmly and taking Barbie's eardrum-piercing laughter in his stride, making interesting conversation about England and his course, even when Barbie talked over him.

Amy politely finished the plate of delicious spinach pasta that a nervous girl had set in front of her, and two minutes later all hell broke loose. After a whole load of shouting, she understood that she'd actually eaten Damien's lunch, and Damien had eaten her chicken salad, against the dietician's orders.

'I'll have you all fired!' Barbie raved as the staff shrank back into the kitchen.

Amy tried to catch Damien's eye, but he was miles away. Amy knew that look. He was daydreaming about football.

After the lunch ordeal was over, Barbie saw her guests to the door. Josh thanked everyone and excused himself. Amy felt like grabbing Damien's arm and making a run for it – she didn't want to waste any more of the afternoon she'd planned with Damien.

First she had to listen to Barbie telling her and Damien to be back at half past two, and how she'd make sure there was a car waiting to take Damien to training and another to take

Amy and Rosay to Orange County. 'Wish I could come shopping with you girls.' Barbie sighed. 'But I'm up to my eyeballs with decorating the guest wing, not to mention the work I'm putting in on organizing the start of season bash. It's a flaming nightmare. And remember you've only got an hour or so before you have to be back, so make the most of it – my old man's got a proper Italian temper!' She gave Damien a playful shove.

The Caseydene courtyard felt hushed in comparison to the sound levels Amy had adjusted to inside. She took Damien's hand and glanced up at the clock. 'Barbie's right. We've only got an hour, and I just want to quickly pop back and change first. Should we skip the sight-seeing and go straight for that ice-cream place?'

Damien leant against a nearby tree and looked worried. 'I can't have stuff like that. Not if I'm training. You heard Carlo.'

'Oh, OK.' Amy shrugged. 'Well, we don't have to do that, then. But let's do *something*. I haven't seen London at all!'

Damien frowned. 'We haven't got *time* to see anything, Ames. Even Barbie said it! I have to be back for training.'

'Yeah, I know ... but we could get out of here for few minutes, couldn't we? Just explore the local streets, maybe? I haven't even seen those!'

'All right. If that's what you want.'

Amy sighed. She thought it was what he wanted, too. But obviously not.

One change of clothes later, she took Damien's hand as they wandered out of the main gates. They'd only walked about three steps when a man leapt out from behind a parked car and waved a camera in their faces, clicking wildly. Amy jumped a mile and yelped, 'Omigod!'

Damien gripped her hand tighter and pulled her along, his face grim. After less than a minute, another three men joined the first one, bending and crouching and snapping Amy and Damien from every angle as they tried to walk innocently along the street. One of the men started yelling questions about when Amy had arrived and whether she was happy to be back with her boyfriend.

Amy shielded her eyes from the scrutiny. 'Does this always happen when you go out?'

'Don't talk.' Damien's face was grim. 'They're dying to catch you saying something they can twist and print.'

'You didn't warn me about this!' Amy couldn't help adding.

'Sssh!' He spoke through gritted teeth. 'I didn't know it would really be like this. I haven't exactly been out much, you know. But Paige told me all about it. I thought she was exaggerating. Just smile.'

'Amy Thornton! You have a face like a wet weekend!' yelled the chatty photographer. The others just kept snapping.

Amy frowned more, even though she tried not to.

'C'mon, give us a grin, Amy!' He stood closer, saying, 'Having boyfriend problems already, eh?'

Amy was ready to tell the photographer what she thought of him, but Damien shot her a warning glance. 'Come on,' he said. He turned down an alleyway and almost broke into a run as he pulled her along and out into the high street at the other end, where they ducked into the nearest shop. It was a large newsagent's, and Damien dragged her behind a shelf of magazines before he stopped, looking around.

'God,' said Amy. 'That was really weird.'

'I think we've lost them,' said Damien seriously.

The way he sounded like something out of a spy film made Amy smile. He caught her eye and grinned back, and all of a sudden they were creasing up uncontrollably, not quite sure what they were laughing at.

'Your life's mad,' Amy told Damien through her laughter.

'So is yours!' Damien pointed to a red-topped paper in front of them that promised 'exclusive photos of newest Sweet Sixteen WAG on the block, Amy Thornton.'

'Wow,' said Amy, picking up the paper. 'How quickly did that happen?' She leafed through the paper.

'I think it's just part of our lives now, Ames. All the media attention. Hey, what's the matter?'

'Look at this!' Amy showed him. It was a photo of her leaving the airport. The headline read 'Trying Too Hard!' and the caption said, 'Schoolgirl WAG-wannabe is in for a shock!' She flicked her eyes over the story and picked out a bit about how out of place she was in her 'dressing-up clothes'. Then there was a quote from 'an unnamed top WAG' agreeing with the reporter's view that her look was 'the equivalent of Coleen's puffa jacket in its pure naffness. We might have our moments, but most of us would wear designer jeans for travelling.' Then the reporter had added, 'Amy had better update her image or Damien will be looking elsewhere, and I wouldn't say no myself! Phwoar!'

Damien laughed. 'That's total rubbish and you know it. You look gorgeous.'

But Amy still found it hurtful. It seemed so unfair. Apart from anything else, there it was in black and white that she needed to worry – that maybe she couldn't compete with effortlessly glamorous girls like Paige Young.

Damien nudged her. 'Hey, those girls are staring at you. Probably wishing they could look as stylish as you.'

Amy looked round. There were three girls of about her age, wearing matching short black skirts and layered vests, standing in a row, just gawping openly in their direction.

Amy realized something about their starstruck expressions. 'Day, they're not staring at me. They're staring at *you*!'

'No way!' Damien grinned, looking over.

One of the girls started giggling and another clutched her friend's arm, gasping loudly. 'Omigod, he smiled at us! Damien Taylor smiled at us!'

'I bet he fancies me!' one of the girls said to her friend, as if Damien couldn't hear her and Amy wasn't standing right there. 'Do you dare me to ask him out?'

'Get lost – you've got no chance. He smiled at *me*!' the friend replied, never once taking her eyes off Damien.

Damien shook his head as if he couldn't believe it and mumbled, 'Come on, Amy, let's go.'

Three pairs of eyes followed them and there was loads more giggling as Damien headed for the door, with Amy following. She couldn't help noticing that the girls' dreamy expressions turned into total daggers – aimed squarely at her – as soon as Damien had gone past.

Outside, there was no sign of any photographers or annoying girls. The high street was bustling with traffic and shoppers. Amy saw a crowded red bus lumber past a tube station, and she realized with a buzz of excitement that she was really in London. All the shopping and sightseeing possibilities of the capital city stretched before her. If only she and Damien had a bit more time to actually *do* something together.

'Rosie hun, sort your little friend out for leaving the house, would you?' Barbie's voice boomed through Caseydene even though Rosay and Amy were standing right next to her. Amy's time with Damien had gone by in a flash, and he'd barely had time to watch her eat the ice cream he'd bought her.

Barbie looked Amy up and down, staring for ages at Amy's clothes and making Amy wonder if she'd dripped ice cream on them. 'Yes, babes, make sure you help her pick out some good clobber – that outfit's worse than the first one! I've cleared it for her to have our usual discount. And if we don't get no freebies, tell 'em we'll go to Pony Club next time, no joke!'

While Amy was so distracted, wondering yet again what exactly was wrong with her clothes, Rosay handed her a baseball cap and some sunglasses.

'Here,' she said. 'It'll probably be a bit of a free-for-all outside the shop.'

'What? Have I got to put these on?' asked Amy, instantly feeling like a total idiot for asking such a silly question. She half expected Rosay to answer, 'No, you're supposed to eat them.' She was sure Asha would have.

But Rosay just said, 'Yeah, if you want to avoid a repeat of what happened earlier.'

Amy grimaced. She'd mentioned the pap incident to Rosay and Barbie, but instead of being sympathetic, they'd both just shrugged in a well-what-do-you-expect sort of way.

Rosay added, 'It's not exactly a disguise, of course – they'll know it's you – but at least you'll look the part, wearing these, and you won't stand out a mile like you do right now.' She smiled kindly. 'Don't worry – once I've kitted you out it'll get better.'

There were two or three photographers waiting outside Caseydene again – possibly the same ones, which made Amy wonder what they did out there all day. She pulled her base-ball cap down and braved the onslaught as she and Rosay cruised past in one of Big Carl's Mercedes, protected by tinted windows, but it wasn't too bad, really. Maybe she was getting used to it already.

The car moved off and she relaxed into the luxury leather, but after a while they stopped at a red light and Amy nearly jumped out of her skin as someone banged at her window. Instinctively, she leant over to open it.

Rosay looked up from her copy of *Grazia*. 'What are you doing?'

Amy was fiddling unsuccessfully with some switches. 'It sounds urgent,' she said.

Rosay shook her head. 'Amy, honestly, I can't believe you. Don't open it! It's paps.'

Amy pulled back and sat on her hands, trying not to feel stupid. 'Are they always like this?'

Rosay shrugged. 'It depends. Right now, you're the hottest new thing in town.' She smiled, but not unkindly. 'It's a slow news week. They'll be tipped off about every move you make.'

Orange County was a large boutique in a row of similar posh-looking shops. A much larger huddle of paps were waiting for them there. Amy hurried past them, tugging at her baseball cap.

At least they didn't follow her into the shop. She loved shopping. She could relax now.

But the shopping experience soon proved traumatic, too. For a start, Amy and Rosay were trailed by a personal shopper, a nervous skinny woman who made suggestions that Rosay attacked with a scary amount of confidence.

'Rubbish. That won't suit her! That wouldn't suit anyone!' was one of the milder comments.

'Uh, sorry, thank you,' Amy muttered more than once, but the personal shopper just smiled at her and Rosay equally, and kept spouting fashion-speak about 'latest lines' and 'asset enhancement'.

About twenty minutes later, the personal shopper was staggering under the weight of an armful of clothes for Amy and Rosay to try on. Amy couldn't get used to having the whole shop to herself – and Rosay. It was so weird not to have to queue and tell the assistant how many items she had, and juggle with Asha and Susi to use part of each other's changing-room allowance.

As soon as the personal shopper had finished hanging the clothes on a series of rails, Rosay rudely waved her away. 'We won't be needing you. I'm really the best judge of what suits us both.'

Amy tried to smile an apology, but the woman strolled away before she could catch her eye.

The changing room itself was amazing. It was huge and softly lit, with gilt-edged mirrors at zany angles, and leather sofas to rest on. There was also a coffee table holding two glasses of recently poured champagne.

Rosay perched on a sofa and picked up a glass. She took

a tiny sip, glancing at Amy. 'You don't want any, do you?'

Amy shook her head. It seemed any time was the right time to drink champagne in this strange new world.

After a few more sips, Rosay got up and started changing. Amy waited for a while, expecting Rosay to give her advice and things to try on, but the girl seemed to be completely focused on herself.

Rosay tried on about a million outfits and posed a lot, pouting, in front of the mirrors. She sang to herself all the time while she did this, warbling some pop hits and even, at one point, Paige's summer hit.

'You've got a good voice,' Amy told her, because it was true. Also because Amy was nervous. She was pretending to join in, tentatively trying on a couple of tops she didn't much like, but feeling well out of her depth. Her Tiffany necklace kept catching on the things she tried and she hoped she wouldn't tear the expensive material.

Rosay looked startled. 'I have not!' Then she smiled sheepishly. 'Have I?'

'Yes, seriously, you have. You sound as good as Paige, singing that song. Well, different from Paige, but still really good.'

'Oh. OK. Thanks.'

Amy felt like kicking herself. She'd obviously said the wrong thing – after all, she knew that Rosay didn't rate Paige very highly. And Rosay seemed to shut down after that, getting through the clothes more quickly, pulling things on and off and barely looking at herself. She seemed lost in thought.

Before long, Rosay had built a tower of discarded clothes on the floor. Amy wasn't sure if that meant she was going to buy them or not.

Meanwhile, Amy spent ages sneakily searching the clothes for price tags. She didn't want to try something on, fall in love with it and then not be able to afford it. She wasn't really sure why she didn't admit that to Rosay, but she didn't want to look stupid. What if Rosay laughed at her or, possibly worse, offered to lend her the money? Amy frowned. She couldn't seem to find any prices at all on the Orange County stock, and she was sure that was a bad sign. She'd probably never be able to pay Rosay back, even if she worked at Water World for the rest of her life.

Rosay dropped another expensive garment on the ground like a rag, and that was when Amy noticed the green skirt Rosay had been wearing, on its own beside the pile. Its hem looked rough and ready at the top, as if it had been hand-sewn by an amateur, and suddenly Amy couldn't resist saying something.

'I like that skirt.' She pointed to it.

'Oh,' Rosay said, putting down the strappy dress she'd been about to try and picking at her nails. 'Thanks.'

Amy decided to keep going. She knew she'd regret it if she didn't. 'Only, it reminds me a lot of the dress you were wearing last night.' She kept her voice light. 'You know. My dress.'

There. She'd said it. What was the worst that could happen? She was wrong, and she'd laugh it off. Why would a girl like Rosay, who lived permanently at Caseydene and had a mum like Barbie and a step-dad like Big Carl, steal her Harvey Nics bargain find and alter it? Badly? It made no sense.

But Rosay totally ignored her, and then said, 'Amy, I meant to tell you. I don't think green is your colour.'

Which made even less sense. Everyone knew that green

clothes went with blonde hair. Green looked fantastic on Amy.

Amy stopped unbuttoning the frilly top she was scouring for price tags. 'Er, OK. So, well, is it? My dress, I mean?'

'What are you talking about? It's a skirt!' Rosay threw a sparkly purple top on to the clothes tower without trying it, and pulled on a black off-the-shoulder one.

Amy wasn't ready to let it go. 'So I can have my dress back, then?' She didn't mean to sound pushy, but Rosay hadn't exactly reassured her.

'Of course you can! But why would you want it? Everyone's seen me wear it now. If there's one thing worse than wearing the same outfit twice, it's being seen in someone else's cast-offs!' She laughed and fiddled with a fastening, not meeting Amy's eye. 'I think we should call it a day. I'll take you to Caffe Americaine for some R&R. I think I'll keep this one on, and the Balenciaga trousers.'

She scooped up the entire clothes tower, leaving the gypsy top and green skirt on the changing room floor. Amy wondered whether to pick them up, but Rosay said, 'Could you give me a hand and take some things off the top of this pile?'

So Amy did, although she was surprised Rosay hadn't summoned the staff to carry the whole lot.

'You go ahead – I'll be there in a second,' Rosay said.

Amy waited patiently at the counter for several minutes. When Rosay finally arrived, she had the personal shopper in tow, staggering slightly under the weight of the rest of the clothes.

The assistant rang up a total that made Amy tremble. She was glad the clothes were all for Rosay, even if it wasn't what

Barbie had in mind for this shopping trip. But Amy knew for sure now that she wouldn't have been able to afford anything here.

Well, at least she'd brought all her best clothes from home. The others were just going to have to get used to Amy's unique style. Maybe she'd wear her baseball cap and shades disguise whenever the footballers' girlfriends were around and they wouldn't know she was the one looking so out of place.

The assistant tapped at the till with French-manicured nails. 'I'll throw in the accessories for you, and the stock you've chosen from the latest lines is also complimentary, of course – it's to be seen in.' Amy was stunned as the total shrank before her eyes. 'And then there's the usual 40 per cent we agreed with Mrs di Rossi.' Tap tap tap.

The amount still made Amy's palms sweat, but it seemed much more manageable. How odd that there should be such huge discounts for people who could clearly afford it.

Rosay clasped a hand to her mouth. 'Oh Amy, I'm afraid I didn't bring my credit card! I hope you don't mind doing the honours this time.'

'*What?*' Amy couldn't possibly have heard her right. Was Rosay suggesting she should pay? What made her even think she *could*? As it happened, she did have a credit card with a pretty good limit – it was tucked safely in the back of her purse. It was her dad's. She'd planned on never using it, though. He'd given it to her for the London trip with special instructions – it was only for dire emergencies. He trusted her.

Rosay said smoothly, 'Don't worry, I promise I'll pay you back way before the bill comes in. And next time will be my treat.'

In the short silence that followed, the personal shopper hummed lightly to herself and rearranged the large paper shopping bags with bright orange cloth handles. The packages almost looked prettier than the clothes inside them.

Rosay cleared her throat. 'Um, Amy? I really won't run away with your money.' She made the word 'money' sound silly, as if Amy was a fool to worry about it. 'You know where I live, remember?' She laughed at her own joke and the personal shopper shuffled the bags together.

Amy sighed and pulled out her purse. She'd explain it to her dad and give him the money to cover it. She entered the PIN she'd memorized and approved the obscene amount as if it was something she did every day. The tissue paper wrapped around the clothes crinkled satisfyingly as she swung Rosay's purchases at her feet and left the shop.

7

Caffe Americaine smelled of strong coffee and deliciously sugary French baking. Amy sat with Rosay on a high silver stool at a retro-style aluminium table. It was all a million miles away from the grey plastic chairs at the chlorine-scented cafe where Susi worked. Susi was the only one of Amy's close friends who hadn't qualified as a lifeguard, and she got stuck with a job Amy would have hated. That was partly because Amy loved hanging around the pool, but mostly because Amy and Asha would go to the cafe after their shifts, when Big Ears their boss couldn't tell them off for chatting any more. Then they'd enjoy tormenting Susi by changing their orders every two minutes and acting totally stuck-up and fussy.

Rosay was doing something similar to the nervous-looking waitress right now, only she wasn't messing around.

'Does the salad contain cress? Because I refuse to entertain *cress*. And only two tomatoes, no more no less. And if there's cucumber, I want it sliced thinly, not diced. I don't want any chunks – of anything. Did you get that?'

The waitress nodded and glanced at the door like she wanted to escape.

'Good. Make sure you get it right. Amy?'

Amy found herself doing the apologetic smiling thing for the second time that day. 'Just a latte. Please.'

Rosay gave her a look.

'I mean, and a salad. Like hers.'

The waitress scuttled away.

Amy wasn't quite sure why she'd changed her order. She really needed to stop feeling so wrong-footed and unsure of herself. Everything felt strange to her, but it was nothing she couldn't handle, surely?

'I'm sorry, Amy. We could have gone somewhere more exclusive, but I wanted to show you the sights.'

'Oh no, this is fine.'

Amy excused herself to use the ladies, wondering what sights Rosay was talking about. She could only see the inside of a dimly lit cafe that wasn't too far from Caseydene, if the tiny amount of time they'd spent in the Mercedes was anything to go by. She thought with a pang about her shortened afternoon with Damien.

When she got back, Rosay snapped her phone shut and gave her a smug smile. 'You're just in time,' she said. 'Here they come. So predictable. I knew they were coming here today after their shopping trip.'

Amy followed Rosay's gaze as a group of girls swished in, carrying armloads of colourful paper shopping bags. They all wore dark glasses and two of them were chatting on pastel-coloured iPhones. It didn't take her long to recognize Paige, Claudette and Kylie. Amy noticed, her heart sinking, that they'd done it again – they looked at once more casual and more stylish than her, like the glamour came naturally to them. How did they *do* that?

They sat at a nearby table, laughing among themselves. Then Claudette got up, stretched and moved towards the door.

A sudden series of flashes lit up outside. Three camera-laden paps crowded round Claudette in the doorway, snapping madly while she smiled, tilted her head prettily and said, 'Oh, guys, you got me!'

A man in a suit came out of the staff area and shooed the paps away as if they were stray cats.

'See how much Claudette posed?' Rosay sniffed as they watched Claudette sit back down with the others. 'She arranged for those paps to be there. And those pictures won't be seen by anyone if she doesn't approve them first – if they don't show her as totally perfect. She's a fake.'

'Really?' said Amy.

'Haven't you noticed? You never see her making funny faces, or in the "celebrity cellulite" pages of the glossies.'

'Yeah, that's true.' Though Amy had assumed it was because Claudette didn't have any cellulite, or ever pulled odd expressions.

'Claudette's not even friends with Paige or Kylie, but she fakes it for the press. It's all about image.'

Amy glanced over again. They certainly looked like friends, chatting together, and not at all what Rosay was describing. On the other hand, she did remember how scathing Claudette had been about Paige.

'And look at all those shopping bags,' Rosay said.

Amy sighed. Part of her wished she could be with those other girls, laughing and carefree. Rosay was tiring her out a bit right now. 'But shouldn't we go over and say hello?' she asked.

Rosay looked at her like she was mad. 'Honestly, Amy, you want to stay away from that lot if you can. Don't let them hook you into their games. All they ever do is spend their husbands' and boyfriends' money.'

'Do you have a job, then?' Amy asked. As soon as the words were out of her mouth she regretted them – she hadn't meant to sound so snide. Or maybe she had, but now she felt embarrassed about it.

Rosay didn't seem to mind. 'Yeah, kind of.'

The waitress arrived with the salads and drinks. Amy thanked her and Rosay scowled.

'So what do you do?' Amy was curious. She couldn't imagine Rosay working for the minimum wage.

'Oh, this and that,' Rosay said vaguely, and busied herself picking at her salad and sipping her drink.

The silence that followed was uncomfortable. 'I work as a lifeguard, every weekend and usually all through school holidays,' Amy said. She launched into a long explanation, complete with descriptions of Susi and Asha and a couple of funny work stories. To her surprise, Rosay warmed up a bit, asking her lots of questions and acting like she was genuinely interested.

'You'll have to use the pool at Caseydene. No one uses it, not now.' She looked wistful. Then she amazed Amy by leaning over and saying quietly, 'I'm sorry. I don't mean to be so miserable all the time, but I miss him, you know?'

'Um ... Actually, no. Who are you talking about? Was it in the papers or anything?'

'Oh, you can't believe a word you read there anyway!'

Amy had thought as much. She barely recognized herself

from the tabloids she'd seen earlier, and that included the photographs.

Rosay put her drink down. 'You're right, though! It always feels like the whole world knows my business. Everyone at the Boroughs thinks they know everything about me, that's for sure. But Mum and Carlo paid people to keep most of this out of the papers.' Rosay took a deep breath. 'Do you remember Marc Frampton?'

Amy wracked her brains.

'Midfielder? Friends with the goalie? Famous for playing up to the camera in press conferences, given half a chance?'

Amy shook her head.

'Transferred from Manchester mid-season year before last, got badly injured in the summer? Is still off recovering, one year on?'

Amy remembered Damien shouting at the telly. 'The one that missed that crucial penalty?'

Rosay's smile reached her eyes. 'Yeah, that was him! And if that's the way you remember him, it's fine by me.' Then her expression hardened. 'Though I tend to think of him as the lying cheat who broke my heart.'

'Wow, I never realized.'

'Me and Marc were a pretty well-kept secret.' She sniffed. 'God, I'm sorry, Amy. You barely know me and you must think I'm such a cow. I know I go on and on about cheating footballers, and that lot.' She nodded in the direction of the laughing group. 'But I have my reasons. Honestly. And I didn't mean to have a go at Damien like that yesterday, but I couldn't help myself. I didn't want you to go through what I did last year.'

Amy thought she understood now. 'Paige Young?' she muttered.

'Yep, you guessed it.' Rosay gave a wry smile and lowered her voice, although as far as Amy could tell, Paige and her friends hadn't even noticed they were there. 'Well, I never proved it. But I knew Marc was seeing someone else – I found all these terrible texts to and from "P", and it had to be her. Everyone knows she's a boyfriend-stealer. She and Trina Santos were best friends – in a band together. I mean, how low can you get?'

Amy nodded. She remembered *that* from the papers.

'When I confronted Marc about it, he dumped me. Just like that.'

The sympathy Amy had felt for Rosay yesterday flooded back in. 'Oh, that must have been awful for you.'

'It was. I can't believe he chose her – that alcoholic – over me.'

'Paige is an alcoholic?'

Rosay nodded absent-mindedly. 'Well, maybe she wasn't at the time, but in the last few weeks I've seen about five pictures of her being "helped into the car" after nights out.' She made a drinking gesture. 'If you know what I mean.'

'But she's only a little bit older than me! How does she even get served?'

'It's easy, Amy, when you're famous! Besides, she probably carries her own booze around in a hip flask or something, and sneaks drinks when no one's looking. Alkies do that.' Rosay waved her arm as if dismissing Paige altogether. Her expression went dreamy. 'Marc was staying at the mews cottage, you know. Same as Damien – Carlo offered him the

place for a while. I met him when he came to use the pool.'
She gave Amy a shy look. 'I used to sneak over to see him
sometimes when I came home. Until the night I picked up his
phone when he wasn't in the room and I found those texts
from *her*.'

'Oh, poor you.' Amy's hand moved instinctively towards
Damien's necklace. So that explained Rosay's actions last
night.

But it couldn't happen to her.

Amy kept feeling for the necklace.

Her neck was bare!

Amy gasped. 'My necklace! It's gone!'

'Are you sure?' Rosay asked.

'I'm sure! Oh no. I've lost it!' Her eyes filled with tears.
'Damien gave that to me. It was . . . It meant a lot . . .' She
couldn't bring herself to say that, since yesterday, she'd been
touching it intermittently as a kind of lucky charm – a reassurance that Damien wouldn't cheat on her. And now it
was gone. It felt like some kind of sign.

'It might have fallen off in the car, or in Orange County.
We'll find it.'

'Won't Orange County be closed now?'

Rosay took out her phone. 'Amy, they were closed before,
when we were there. Don't worry, honestly. I'll phone Mum
and get her to put a call through.'

Amy sniffed. 'Thanks. I should check in here, too.' She
scanned the floor by her chair. Then she remembered she'd
been to the ladies earlier. 'I'll be right back!'

She left Rosay talking to her mum and ran, shoving the
swing door hard in her hurry.

But it resisted and she heard someone say, 'Ow!'

Oh no, she'd whacked the door right into someone!

'I'm so sorry!' she called, waiting a bit and then pushing the door more tentatively. It opened and she stepped gingerly into the room. 'Only I've lost something and . . . Oh.'

It was Paige Young. She was red in the face, rubbing her side and looking flustered. She glanced at Amy and looked away, quickly tucking something into her pocket.

8

'Oh, hi,' Amy mumbled.

Paige dropped her arms as if to shield her side. Then she seemed to relax a bit.

'Hi, Amy. I saw you over in the corner with Rosay – I was going to say hello but it seems you've run into me anyway.' Her laugh was nervous. She didn't sound as friendly as she had yesterday.

'I'm really sorry about hitting you with the door. I was –'

'It's OK, it's my fault for standing right behind it. Did you say you'd lost something?'

'Yeah, a necklace. I wanted to check in here. It's . . . it's from Damien.' Even to herself, Amy sounded like she was trying to make a point.

Paige gave her an odd look. 'OK, but what does it look like? Gold? Silver?' She started searching the ground. 'Anything on it?'

'Silver. With a heart pendant, studded with diamonds. Damien gave it to me.' Amy couldn't stop herself.

'Right.' Paige kept looking. 'I can't see anything, can you?'

'No,' Amy admitted, managing to stop herself saying any

more about Damien. She was being ridiculous! Why didn't she just come straight out with it: 'Paige, I've heard about you, so don't get any ideas about stealing my boyfriend.' Instead she said, 'It's OK, don't worry. Thanks for looking. I'm sure I'll find it.' She tried to believe that.

'No problem. I hope you do.' Paige hesitated with one hand ready to open the door. 'Oh, by the way, Amy ... I know you and Damien are staying with Rosay's family right now and I don't want to make things awkward for you. But I wanted to say ...' She glanced around and took a deep breath. 'Well, you shouldn't necessarily believe everything Rosay tells you. She's not big on telling the truth. Or she, kind of, sees things in her own way, if I'm being generous.'

'Oh,' said Amy, feeling more confused as the day went on. These girls were bitchy, that was for sure.

'Look, it's a long story, but, well, some of the girls don't really want her around. Kylie, especially –'

'Kylie?' Amy couldn't hide her surprise. Kylie had seemed so harmless. Even Rosay had said so.

'Oh, she thinks she's protecting me! Kylie's so sweet – she'd be the perfect flatmate, if only it didn't mean having to share with Poshie as well.'

For a crazy fleeting moment Amy thought she was talking about Victoria Beckham, and maybe it showed on her face because Paige laughed.

'Poshie is short for Poshie Pug – Kylie's pet. He's a gorgeous little dog, and he's super stylish, like Kylie. She spoils him rotten – he has his own room at Spooky Towers. That's what Kylie calls our building, because it's at 13 Elm Street. You know, like *Nightmare on Elm Street*?' She shrugged and smiled.

'Poshie lives in the room that used to be Rosay's, back when I shared with her and Trina.'

'Oh, right,' Amy said. She was increasingly glad her friendship with the twins was so simple.

'Anyway, listen, there's this small dinner party thing at Johann's a week on Wednesday – that's Kylie's boyfriend.'

Amy laughed. 'Don't worry, Damien would never forgive me if I didn't know who he was.' Johann Haag had been one of Damien's heroes for years. He was from the Netherlands and was a winger like Damien. Amy had spent hundreds of Sunday afternoons flicking through Asha's fashion magazines while Damien rewound and replayed Johann Haag's moves in his World Cup DVD collection.

'Yeah.' She smiled. 'So Kylie and Johann would love it if you and Damien could come. Me and Scotty are going. I hope.'

It all sounded very coupley, and not at all like the kind of party where Paige would be any threat to her and Damien.

Paige shifted about. 'But, it's just that . . . er, you really can't bring Rosay this time. Don't get me wrong – I didn't mind her turning up at Scotty's yesterday, even with that scene she made. I'm over it, you know, even if *she* can't seem to let it go.'

Amy wondered what there was for Paige to be over, when surely Rosay had been the wronged party over the Marc Frampton affair.

'But if you tell Rosay, she'll try to invite herself along, and I know she can be really forceful. And Kylie will mind, even if she's too nice to say directly. So . . .'

'Oh, no, right, I get it,' Amy said. This was too confusing.

She had no idea who to trust. But at least she had someone she could rely on – Damien worshipped Johann and Amy knew he'd love to go. 'I'll check with Damien. I'm sure it'll be fine and we'd love to come, thanks.'

'Great. I'll tell Kylie. She wanted to ask you herself yesterday at Scotty's party. But first she couldn't get you without Rosay, and then she didn't want to interrupt you with Damien.' Paige's eyes sparkled. 'Of course Kylie asked Johann to ask Damien, but you know what boys are like – especially ours, all obsessed with football. I bet he forgot the second she told him.'

Amy smiled. Paige was so easy-going and friendly. It was hard to believe she was the evil boyfriend-stealer Rosay kept telling her about.

'Well, I hope you find your necklace.'

Paige swung out of the room.

Amy had one more unsuccessful search for the necklace and then went back to where Rosay was still talking away on her phone.

Rosay jumped when she saw Amy.

What was it with everyone? She could have sworn that first Paige and now Rosay had looked completely guilty. But about what? Amy told herself she was imagining it all. Having to watch every move she made was making her paranoid and suspicious.

'OK, yep. Will do. Bye.' Rosay clipped her phone shut and turned back to Amy. 'Any luck?'

Amy shook her head.

'It's not at Orange County. Mum had them scour the floors for it. Are you sure you were wearing it when you went out this morning?'

'Yeah, I was. I always wear it.'

'I don't remember seeing any necklace, to be honest. Never mind, it'll turn up.'

Rosay pushed the salad plate aside and put her phone in her bag. 'Come on, I think we should go. The others left a minute ago and I said I'd show you the sights, didn't I? We'll probably find them in this private members' bar I know. You can go to the spa tomorrow, if you're worried about the toxins.'

Amy hesitated. Rosay seemed to be suggesting that they would follow the other girls around, and Amy wasn't sure about doing that. It seemed . . . underhand, or something. The conversation with Paige had unnerved her, but she couldn't exactly explain that to Rosay.

'But won't the training be over by now? It's been ages. I mean, I really wanted to spend some time with Damien today.'

Rosay sniffed. 'You'll be lucky. Carlo will turn on the floodlights and keep going until he drops. Besides, the boys will probably all go out together when it's over. Carlo encourages the whole male bonding thing. That's what they do.' She seemed to be reading Amy's thoughts because she added, 'Even Damien, Amy. He's been getting home really late this past month or two.' She widened her eyes. 'Oh, hasn't he told you?'

Amy decided not to say what she was thinking, which was, 'Of course he's told me! But *I'm* here now. It's different. He *wants* to see me!' She decided there was probably no persuading Rosay on the subject of footballers who actually liked and respected their girlfriends. Instead, she said, 'Well, in any case, I want to go back. You go on without me. I don't mind, honestly. I'll find my own way.'

Rosay bristled. 'No, no. I'll come with you.' She sucked in a non-existent stomach. 'I could probably do with using the gym, and if I leave you on your own you'll probably start inviting the paps to join you for a photo opportunity!' She smiled as she handed Amy a tall leather wallet. 'The bill. You pay over there, on the way out. I'll bring my credit card next time, I promise.'

The amount was very much smaller this time. Amy didn't worry so much about typing in her dad's PIN. It just felt like numbers, anyway – not like spending real money. She had cash in her purse, withdrawn from her savings to use when she got to London, and she hadn't touched it yet. In fact, at this rate, her savings would last all summer.

As Amy paid, she was dazzled by a sudden explosion of flashing light. She squinted towards the cafe window, which was almost obscured by paparazzi pointing their cameras at her.

Great. She wasn't wearing her hat or her sunglasses, she was still in the clothes Barbie said were even worse than her earlier outfit, she'd lost her necklace and, worst of all, she was sure her face was contorting hideously at the unexpected onslaught of bright light.

She sighed. The gossip columns would have a field day tomorrow.

9

Amy fully expected Rosay to breeze into the mews cottage with her, like she had the day before. She was slightly worried about it – after all, Damien had made it clear he didn't rate his manager's step-daughter, and now Paige had planted doubts in her mind, too. Although Amy wasn't sure how much to trust Paige, either.

But when the Mercedes pulled up outside Caseydene, Rosay got out of the car and wandered off. 'See you later.'

'Oh, OK. Bye.' Amy remembered she was still holding the shopping bags. She had to admit, she liked the weight of them in her hand. 'Wait – don't forget these!'

'Oh, yeah.' Rosay took the bags, peered into each one, selected two and handed the rest to Amy. 'Here. These are yours.'

'What?' But Amy hadn't chosen any clothes! 'No, they're all yours.'

Rosay shrugged. 'I know, but I like sharing clothes with my friends.' She smiled at Amy. 'Besides, Mum's going to kill me if she finds out I didn't choose you any clothes after all that. You have to take them.' She gestured to the bags. 'And wear them. Please? The vultures will be after you again tomorrow.

It's time you got some good shots of yourself out there. You're gorgeous! You're easily better-looking than stupid Paige Young, and I'd much rather the papers were filled with pictures of you than of *her*.'

Amy panicked. 'But I don't even know if they'll fit me!'

'Course they will – I made sure they were all loose on me. You've only been here five minutes – don't go all anorexic on me already! Hey, why don't you come over and use the pool tomorrow, if you're worried about your weight?'

Amy wanted to say that she wasn't remotely worried about her weight – she was proud of her athletic build – but Rosay was already halfway up the path to the main house.

Amy clasped the shopping bags. So she had some new clothes after all. A terrible part of her wondered whether Rosay was still going to give her the money for them. Maybe she'd ask her tomorrow. She sighed.

She decided to see what Damien thought of it all. She was dying to talk to him. But it turned out that Rosay was right. Damien wasn't at home and he wasn't answering his phone, which meant he was probably still at training.

Amy decided to keep the clothes in their Orange County bags by the door. She'd give them back to Rosay tomorrow and explain to Barbie that she'd bought the wrong size or something, so that Rosay didn't get into trouble. Barbie might be loud, but she didn't seem the sort to get all that angry with her daughter.

Amy made herself a cup of tea and a sandwich from some supplies that had mysteriously appeared in the kitchen while she'd been out. The wholemeal bread and lean cooked chicken had to be part of the new Damien diet regime.

She phoned her mum and dad for a catch-up, and then Susi and Asha for an even longer chat.

Her dad asked her if she was eating properly and what formations Carlo had talked about. Her mum laughed about Barbie and gasped at Amy's description of Orange County. Amy didn't mention having used the credit card. She thought she'd wait until she had the money from Rosay.

Susi told her to be careful and that both Rosay *and* Paige sounded like bad news and she should come home to her *real* friends. Though they might visit her first. She said her bachelor uncle in London was feeling lonely and wouldn't mind a visit from his nieces – if only they didn't have to work.

Asha said she'd visit right now if it wasn't for the fact that Uncle Dinesh always left his incredibly smelly socks around the flat, and anyway, when was Amy taking her shopping? Then Amy heard all their news about eccentric customers in the cafe and fit boys pretending to drown to get Asha to give them the kiss of life.

Amy ended up laughing till her sides ached.

After that, she tried Damien again but there was still no reply. She settled in front of the TV and flicked through the channels, trying not to feel lonely.

It was around ten when she got a text from Damien: 'Out with the lads – sorry, Big C's orders! Love you, miss you. xxx'.

She texted back that she loved him too and she missed him too, then looked through a copy of *Vogue* and imagined being able to afford all the outfits inside. Claudette Harris always looked as though she'd stepped straight from the pages of a glossy magazine like this. She was a professional fashion icon as far as the media were concerned.

At eleven thirty, another text came through: 'Running late. Sorry! Don't wait up! xxx'.

But she thought she would. She'd surprise him. It was only her second night in London – how late could he be?

At two in the morning a late-night film finished and her eyelids were amazingly droopy.

The display on the DVD player said 05:10 a.m. when she felt the soft weight of a blanket being tucked around her and she vaguely detected Damien's familiar after-shave. She groaned and struggled to say hello, but her eyelids were too heavy. He kissed her forehead and then he was gone, and she thought she might be dreaming anyway.

Amy woke up in a total grump. How could soft leather be so uncomfortable? Her body felt crumpled, like it needed some straightening irons to sort it out. She performed a whole series of limbering up exercises, stretching as much as she could, but it wasn't helping. A swim was definitely the only solution.

But first she wanted to find Damien. Had he even come home last night? She wasn't sure.

She walked over to the kitchen and immediately spotted a yellow Post-it note stuck to the fridge. Damien's writing was more of a scrawl than it had been on Saturday's notes. It said, 'I'm sorry! Deffo got Monday off! That's today! WAKE ME UP!!! xxx'.

She hesitated by his door. But if she hadn't dreamt the fact that he'd come home at five in the morning, then it was far too early to wake him. He'd only have slept for about three hours.

And anyway, part of her felt irrationally angry with him for leaving her on her own all evening. Let him wake up to an empty house and wonder where *she* was!

Amy gathered her swimming things and strode over to the main house. But when she got there, she lost her confidence. What if it was too early to knock? Rosay had told her more than once that she could use the pool, but she hadn't actually showed her where it was.

Amy badly wanted a swim.

She took a deep breath and rapped at the door.

A tall woman with a stern face answered, rubbing floury hands on her jeans. 'Yes?'

'I'm, er, Amy. I'm staying in the mews cottage. I've come to use the pool. Er . . . Rosay said it was OK.'

'And Mr di Rossi, he say is OK too?' The woman had a heavy accent that Amy guessed might be Eastern European. 'I learn early, I no believe Rosay,' she added grimly. 'She get me in trouble.'

Amy was slightly surprised that the woman was being so blunt.

'Who is it, Eva?' a familiar voice boomed in the distance. 'Oh, Amy! How nice to see you!'

It was Barbie, wearing a very short and almost see-through silky negligee.

'Hi . . . er,' Amy said, not sure what to call her, or where to look.

'Don't tell me you've come for your meals again!' Barbie cackled. 'Carlo says he's getting food sent over from now on, so that you two lovebirds can eat in private.'

'She want to use the pool,' Eva said, stalking off without a backward glance and leaving Amy with Barbie.

'Oh! Well, of course you can, babe! I'd suggest getting Rosay to go with you, only I'm sure she's sound asleep. All shopped out! I heard you had fun hitting Orange County yesterday?'

Amy opened and closed her mouth, but Barbie didn't leave her a big enough gap to explain.

'Course you did! I knew I was right. Shame about your necklace, but I'm sure it will turn up!' She gestured to her negligee, which shimmered in a see-through sort of way. 'You'll have to excuse us.' She didn't look remotely embarrassed about it. 'We're not early risers in this house – except Carlo, of course. He's been off worrying at that club for hours already.'

'Wow, doesn't he sleep at all?' Amy wondered, and then she shifted nervously, thinking it must have sounded like an odd thing for her to say. She'd been thinking of his late night with Damien.

Barbie gave her trademark extra-loud laugh. 'That's what I always say – he gets up at dawn! But at least he's always tucked up proper early, mind you. He was out like a light before nine last night! He's a day person, not a night owl . . .'

Amy's mind wandered as Barbie kept talking. So Big Carl hadn't been out with the boys after training.

She tried to calm herself down. It didn't mean that Damien was lying. Hadn't Rosay said something about male bonding sessions? She must have meant among the team members, but not including their boss.

'Come with me, I'll show you to the pool!'

Barbie clipped down a long corridor in her fluffy stiletto slippers and Amy hurried after her.

'You're lucky you caught me, babe – I'm not normally up at this time either, and who knows whether Eva would have just sent you packing! I really must do something about her. But no, I'm so stressed right now, I don't have time to sort out the staff.'

'Ah,' Amy said. The pool was starting to seem a very long way away.

'Yeah, I'm finishing off overseeing the decorating in the guest wing. And I'm in charge of the whole start-of-season charity ball for the Boroughs. Just like that – last minute – it's all down to me! Well, it always was down to me, of course, but I had a party planner, you know. She was only the best! And only seven months pregnant, so you'd think there was plenty of time to plan a party and then pop a sprog, wouldn't you?'

There was a pause while Barbie looked at Amy expectantly.

'Er, yeah,' Amy said.

'Well, you're wrong! You and me both! She dropped proper early and now look at the mess I'm in!' Barbie pushed several doors and Amy followed her into the main courtyard. Amy could see the path to her cottage again – they'd obviously gone a long way round. 'The other party planners are all booked and I don't trust them anyway. She won't even answer her phone, I can't work out what she'd sorted and what she hadn't, and I'll tell you, babe, it's beginning to look like she hadn't done much of anything! No wonder she's avoiding me! I don't even know who to get in touch with at the Royal Clinic!'

Amy felt confused. 'Is that a hospital?'

'Yes, the party's a fundraiser, you see. The Royal is a private clinic for cosmetic surgery – they do some amazing stuff there. They did a good job on my boobs the year before last, even though I've got that problem with the left one. And they did my eyelids last year. Look. Great, ain't they?' Barbie stopped, shut her eyes and poked her head out towards Amy.

'Oh,' said Amy, relieved that it was Barbie's eyelids she was supposed to admire. 'Yes. Great.'

Barbie opened her eyes again. 'Well, I can't get a hold of the Royal at all. It's a shambles!'

'Ah,' said Amy. 'It sounds bad.'

'It is. It's a train wreck, I'm telling you, babe.' Barbie sighed. 'Well, here we are. Through here.' She gestured to a separate building off the courtyard, then she opened a door and led the way.

Amy almost gasped. It was amazing. They were standing in a foyer that looked a lot like the entrance to a sports centre, but without the crowds and sweaty smells. On one side there was a glass-walled gym area with various machines and fitness gadgets. On the other, also behind glass, was an indoor tennis court. But, best of all, right in the middle, past some groups of tables and chairs, was a medium-sized pool. Its blue colour glistened invitingly at Amy and her heart swelled with happiness.

'Here you go, babe. The pool!' Barbie announced. 'Give us a shout if you need anything. Have fun.'

'Thank you so much,' Amy said, and to prove that she really meant it, she found herself adding, 'And maybe I can help you with your party thing sometime? Me and my friends were in charge of the end-of-holiday-club disco at Water World last Easter.' The she realized how ridiculous that must sound. 'I mean, I know it's not the same thing, but I know a bit about entertaining difficult crowds and keeping party-goers happy. Maybe I could help? Argh!'

Barbie had thrown her arms around her. 'Oh, babe, that would be fabulous! You're such a lovely girl!' she gushed. 'I'm so glad Rosay has a friend like you after everything that's happened. And your boyfriend's a bit of all right, too, know what I mean? You want to hold on to that one!'

Her laugh echoed around the sports complex as she left Amy to enjoy one of the many perks of her summer holiday. It was just a shame she had to do it alone.

10

Amy cut across the water, deciding to enjoy the luxury of having a whole pool to herself. She swam thirty delicious laps before she noticed out of the corner of her eye that there was someone on the tennis court.

Amy's heart lurched. For a split second she thought it was Damien – maybe he'd come over to see her and apologize for coming home late. Amy hauled herself on to the edge of the pool to get a better look. She knew immediately that it wasn't her boyfriend. This man wasn't messing around – he was a tennis pro. Everything about him was precise and determined as he served ball after ball accurately over the net. She couldn't help but admire his gorgeously muscular legs.

The man turned and tipped the tennis racquet towards her as if to say hello.

It was Josh! Amy gave a tiny wave back, feeling her cheeks grow hot. She hoped he hadn't noticed her checking him out, which was kind of what she'd been doing, even though she hadn't meant to.

She stretched her arms and legs and decided that the swimming had done its job.

A few minutes later, Amy wandered out of the pool area.

She'd showered, changed back into the Juicy Couture tracksuit she'd got at TK Maxx and was rubbing her damp hair on a towel. She hesitated outside the entrance to the court, wondering if it would be rude to leave without waving goodbye to Josh.

But he saw her, lowered his racquet and walked over, stepping into the main foyer of the sports complex. 'Hi, Amy. You're up early.'

'Hi,' she said. 'Just keeping up with the swimming routine.' She felt oddly shy.

'You're a pretty good swimmer.'

'Thanks – years of lifeguard training! You're a pretty good tennis player.' Amy hid her face in her towel, sure she was blushing. She hoped she sounded friendly and not flirty.

He smiled. 'I haven't played for a while. My uni's more into team sports, and I'm a bit rusty. But Carlo generously offered me the use of the court while I'm on this work placement. It's a good thing because I'm totally lost in London and I haven't even managed to find a sports centre yet.'

'It's a big city,' Amy said. 'I don't know if Damien's had a chance to see any of it either.' *Well, not in daylight anyway*, she thought to herself, and immediately felt guilty.

'I know.' His eyes crinkled as if he might be laughing at her, but kindly. 'Carlo wants me to help Damien get settled. It's kind of my first assignment. I'm supposed to go and talk to him today.'

'You'll be lucky – he's still asleep!' Amy blurted, and immediately remembered Josh officially worked for Damien's boss. What if she caused more trouble for him? 'I mean, sorry . . . I don't actually know if *right now* he's . . .'

'Hey, don't worry,' Josh said. 'The session's later. I don't think Damien even knows about it yet – Carlo likes to spring things on his players, keep them on their toes. I came early to take advantage of the court.'

'Oh.' It occurred to Amy that it was supposed to be Damien's day off. Again. Did Big Carl ever really let his players have time off? When was she supposed to have time with her boyfriend? Her idyllic summer with Damien wasn't going at all according to plan.

'Hey, are you OK?' Josh's eyes were full of concern.

'Um. Yeah, sure.' Amy suddenly worried that if she said any actual words she might cry.

Josh's voice was gentle. 'Look, I know I'm only a student, and mostly in team psychology at that. But I've already passed some counselling qualifications and I've done some one-to-one sessions. I grew up with two highly rated psychologists for parents. I know how this stuff works – that's why Carlo gave me the placement.'

'Uh huh,' Amy mumbled.

'What I'm trying to say is, if you want to talk about it, I'm a good listener. It would be confidential, of course.'

He sounded so sincere and sombre that she couldn't help herself. She burst out laughing.

He looked confused.

'Oh, I'm sorry,' she said. 'I'm being weird. It's nothing serious, though, honestly! It's just that everything since I got here, well. It's nothing like I expected.'

'Really? What did you expect?'

Was he starting a 'one-to-one session' with her? Amy put her head on one side and wondered whether she should speak at all.

It was Josh's turn to laugh. 'I'm asking out of interest. As a friend. I'm not going to psychoanalyse you.' His eyes twinkled. 'Much. I can't help doing it a little. It's the way I was brought up, I suppose. But sports psychology isn't really about that, anyway – it's about enhancing performance and overcoming injuries. Visualization, relaxation, that kind of thing. As well as integrating new players, making them feel part of the team.'

'Wow, I had no idea it was that complicated. So what's your course like? Is it the same as sports science?' That was what Amy wanted to study, after science A Levels. She'd thought about being a physiotherapist or a trainer, but Josh was making sports psychology sound interesting too.

'I'll tell you. But only if you tell me more about what you meant before. I could probably tell you a couple of stories too.' He lowered his voice. 'Between you and me, and this isn't a *professional* opinion, you understand . . .' He leant closer. 'I think this family's slightly crazy.'

Amy pretended to look horrified and Josh gave an easy laugh.

'Mind you, this level of wealth is liable to send anyone off their rocker.' He glanced in the direction of the tables. 'So what do you reckon? Should we sit and have a chat? I don't want to go back to the main house anyway. Barbie scares me.'

Amy giggled at the thought of this tall, toned, muscle-bound guy being worried about the petite Barbie. 'Yeah, OK.'

So they sat and talked. He told her all about his college and the modules he was taking in coaching and research, and Amy thought it sounded brilliant. Then she told him bits and pieces of what had happened since she'd arrived in London, and he listened and asked lots of typical counsellor-like questions. Amy had seen a counsellor for a while last year when she was learning to cope with her mother's chemo. She knew all their tricks, the way they asked questions that made you open up and think about yourself. Listening to Josh lapsing so easily into counsellor-talk nearly made her laugh again, but it was also nice to have someone entirely non-judgemental to talk to.

She managed not to tell Josh anything about Damien, though. It would have felt a bit like betraying him, somehow, especially since they had that session later. She wondered how Damien would take it, being forced by his manager to talk to a lad his own age about his inner feelings. She could just imagine the trapped look on his face when he found out.

The thought made her smile and miss him yet again, even though she had to admit that the guy in front of her was seriously gorgeous and, if it wasn't for Damien, she'd most likely have a major crush on Josh by now.

She wasn't sure how long they'd chatted, but by the time she set off for the mews cottage she felt much calmer, like she could cope with anything. She thought it was probably late enough now to wake Damien up and sort things out, clear the air between them.

Leaving Josh practising his serve again, she headed across the courtyard. Then she stopped short because she couldn't quite believe what she was seeing.

A bejewelled, highly glamorous person was coming out of the main house, calling, 'See you later, Rosay darling! *Mwah mwah!*'

It was Claudette Harris. Saying goodbye to Rosay as if they were best friends!

But Claudette and Rosay hated each other – didn't they?

Amy froze in confusion as Rosay shut the door. Claudette turned, noticed her and did a royal wave in her direction. 'Amy!' she called.

Claudette strode towards her, covering ground very quickly with her impossibly long, model-like legs. She had the latest Hermès Birkin bag slung over her arm and some very large Chanel sunglasses on. 'I was on my way to see you.'

'Me?'

'Yes. Would you like to come with me to the spa this afternoon?'

'Er . . . *me*?'

Claudette looked her up and down. 'Yes. You. They do let babies in, you know, there's no lower age limit.' She tinkled a laugh at what she obviously thought was a great joke. 'Or have you already been today? That's an interesting hair-style.'

Amy touched the ratty, damp ends of her hair self-consciously. 'I've been swimming in the pool here.'

'Aw, how nice,' Claudette said vaguely. 'You'll like the spa, then. It has a larger pool than Rosay's poxy puddle. But you don't have to do anything so . . . chlorinated if you don't want to. I've booked some treatments for us. You know, the standard kind they offer at all places with pools.'

'Treatments?' They didn't offer those at Water World. They had fun slides, a wave machine and a kiddie fountain shaped like a turtle. She felt embarrassed just thinking about it.

'Hydrotherapy, massage, stone therapy,' Claudette continued, glancing back at the house. 'Don't worry, I've cleared it with your babysitter.'

'My what?'

Claudette laughed. 'Rosay said she'd lend you anything you need, darling. I'll pick you up myself. See you at two thirty!' She swished away towards a large black car that was waiting for her.

Amy's head was full of questions.

Like: what was stone therapy?

And: why was Claudette friends with Rosay, even though Paige had suggested – no *stated* – yesterday that the girls didn't want Rosay around?

Also: why had she agreed to this on Damien's day off?

At least she could answer the last question. Damien had his session with Josh this afternoon anyway, so it wasn't like the two of them could go anywhere.

She let herself into the mews cottage. The bedroom doors were still closed but the kitchen wasn't how Amy had left it. Someone – the cleaner, or Eva, perhaps – had clearly been round with more supplies. A hamper of healthy-looking food rested on the counter top, together with a folded tabloid newspaper.

She wondered about waking Damien up now, but she was starving from the swim and the hamper looked tempting. She selected a bag of banana chips and shook out the newspaper with her other hand. She sat down and put her feet up on the sofa, tucking into her snack and leafing through the paper.

Then she froze.

A photo of Damien smiled up at her, next to a similar one of Scott White – they were familiar headshots that Amy recognized from the team website. Below them was a picture that was slightly blurred by light bouncing off the window of Caffe Americaine. With a rush of embarrassment, Amy recognized herself, her face contorted and eyes squinting, her feet surrounded by Orange County shopping bags, her look decidedly dowdy. Next to her photo was one of Paige Young in her pop-star days, looking incredible in a figure-hugging black dress.

Great. Just great.

She looked closer.

The main headline read, 'Boroughs Boys Brawl!' And in smaller lettering, it said, 'Could Taylor and White be on the same Paige?'

Amy's photo had a caption: 'The newest Boroughs WAG gets FLASH with the cash ... Make the most of it, Amy Thornton!'

Amy's head swam and her stomach churned. What was this about?

She read it once, shook her head in disbelief and read it again.

'Our inside source saw DAMIEN TAYLOR, 18, hottest new player with Royal Boroughs, out 'n' about last night with BLONDE STARLET Paige Young, 17 – but where was Paige's fiancé and Taylor's team-mate, the infamous 22-year-old striker SCOTT WHITE? Is Paige about to show White the RED CARD and bring in Taylor as a sub? Boroughs boys, please don't fight! It's not worth it – we've heard recently that Paige's true love is her booze! Meanwhile, Taylor's childhood sweetheart Amy, 16, visiting from her West Yorkshire home and blissfully ignorant, was snapped enjoying the WAG life-style. Don't get too comfy, little Amy!'

The article went on a bit about Amy and her clothes and how out of place and innocent she looked. Amy stopped reading and threw the paper down.

Damien was seen out and about with Paige? *Last night?*

She jumped up and stormed into Damien's room, not caring how much noise she made.

'Damien! Wake up NOW!'

The bed was made, the room was tidy. Damien wasn't there.

11

Each time Amy tried Damien's phone, it went straight to voicemail. The third time, she spotted his phone on the coffee table in the corner of the room. She picked it up, but it was switched off. She threw both handsets at the sofa in frustration. Where was he? How could he do this to her?

She paced up and down, searching the cottage for clues and wondering whether to switch his phone on and look at his messages, like Rosay had done with Marc Frampton's phone. But that seemed a step too far.

Instead, she reminded herself that Damien's note was still on the fridge – the note he must have written last night. So he must have come home. But he had gone out again? Maybe to *Paige's* house? She tried to push away all the evil thoughts that were making her eyes prickle with angry tears.

Her phone rang and she dived for it, finding it half-buried by a leather cushion.

'Amy! Are you OK?'

It was Asha. Amy sniffed. 'Yes,' she said, but her voice wobbled. 'OK, no! Did you see the paper?'

'Susi came to find me – she saw someone reading it in the cafe. She spotted Damien before she recognized you. That photo looked nothing like you!' She squealed. 'And it was in *all* the papers – the pic, I mean, not the gossip thing. All that shopping! Wow! You might even make *Heat* magazine! What, Susi?' There was a pause. 'Yeah, right. About that. I'm seriously going to kill Damien! I'm going to chop him up and – *What?* Listen, Susi says we've only got about ten seconds before Big Ears goes on the prowl. Here she is with the Party Political Broadcast from the Sensible Squad.'

'Asha, shut up! Amy?'

'Susi!' Amy clutched the phone as a tear escaped down her cheek.

'Right, Amy, you have to remember that these papers publish any old rubbish. And it's called "gossip", remember? You can't believe a word of it. Have you got that?'

'Yes.' Amy's tears instantly began to dry up. Sometimes it was great to be bossed around by Susi.

'So. Has Damien seen it? Is he there? What did he say?'

'No. He . . .'

'Did you kick him out? Because I totally understand that, but you should listen to his side of it first and I bet you didn't.'

'Susi, I can't kick him out. I'm the visitor here. I'd . . . I'll have to come home.' Amy couldn't believe she was saying these things. What had happened to her perfect summer, and so soon?

'Well, promise me you'll talk to Damien first!' Susi said. 'In the meantime I'll restrain Asha cos she's practically on the next train down there with her man-murdering kit. That's still Plan B, though. Let us know how it goes! Anyway, we've got to go or Big Ears will kill us first.'

'OK.'

Amy heard a click behind her. The door.

Damien was home.

'Amy?' Susi said. 'This is Damien we're talking about, remember? It's going to be all right. He loves you.'

'He's here,' Amy half-whispered into the phone.

'Good. Ask him about it.' Susi hung up.

Damien stood in the doorway. He was wearing a tracksuit and he looked sweaty and out of breath and gorgeous. Amy's stomach swirled with a mix of emotions, like relief, anger and a sudden urge to throw her arms around him. But the anger won.

'Where have you been?' She didn't even try to take the accusing note out of her voice.

He shrugged casually. 'I went for a run. I woke up and you weren't here so I thought I'd get some extra training in. Where have *you* been?'

She had to admit, he looked like he was telling the truth. 'But what time did you get home last night?'

'Far too late. But you still could have woken me up this morning. Didn't you see my note?'

'I saw a lot more than that!'

He looked puzzled. 'What do you mean?'

She gestured to the paper she'd thrown at the sofa. 'Have you read that?'

'No. Why?' He started to walk towards it but she stepped in front of him to stop him. She wanted to talk to him first, before he knew what he needed to cover for. Maybe she wanted to catch him out. She couldn't believe she was thinking that.

'Who were you with last night?' Amy held her breath. This was it. She wasn't sure she wanted to hear the answer.

'Why? You can't believe that stuff, Amy! You know that. They've been leaving me a paper here every day, even before the food baskets, but I try not to look at it any more. Last time I did, I read that I was twenty-one and drove a BMW. Yesterday they said you had no fashion sense, and we all know how wrong that is!'

She ignored his smile. 'OK, but I still want to know who you were with last night.'

He stopped smiling and folded his arms. 'You're doing it again!'

'Doing what?'

'Sounding like a jealous girlfriend, like you did on Saturday!' Damien's eyes flared. 'What does that paper say? Let me see.'

She blocked his way again. 'First. Tell me. Who you were with last night.'

They glared at each other.

Damien mimicked her tone in his reply. 'I. Was out. With the team. Like I said.' He sighed. 'Look, Amy. You know I really wanted to go out with you yesterday, and last night, but I couldn't. I know it seems like I'm messing you about, but I'm not. I'm trying to do everything by the book – it's my big break! Big Carl ordered this team night out. Maybe it wasn't supposed to be such a late night, but you know how these things go.'

'So was Big Carl with you?' She knew he wasn't. She wasn't sure why she was doing this – testing Damien, playing games. They didn't need to have conversations like this; they trusted each other. But it all felt different now. Paige Young was so glamorous and it was obvious Damien liked her – who knew what he might do now that his life had changed so much?

Damien tightened his folded arms. 'No, he wasn't. Can I go now? I need a shower and you need to calm down.'

He was halfway to the bathroom when she spoke again. 'So who was with you?'

He sighed. 'Amy, come *on*.'

'Damien, just tell me.'

'I just did. The lads. The team.'

'Any girls?'

Damien shrugged. 'Yeah, a couple of the girlfriends turned up later.'

Amy pushed aside the thought that Damien could have invited *her*, but he seemed to read her mind anyway.

'It wasn't planned. They just turned up in the same place as us. I don't think they were supposed to be there, and anyway, it was too late to call you by then.'

She barely paused. She needed to keep asking questions. 'So was Paige Young there?'

He frowned. 'Yes.'

'And was Scott White there?'

He looked at the ceiling, at the floor, at the door, but not at her. 'He'd left by then. Why? Is that thing about Scott and Paige?'

Amy's heart sank. There it was. Guilt. He looked guilty.

Her anger was suddenly replaced with desperation. She wanted to throw herself at him and say something pathetic like, 'Please promise you're not cheating on me and you never will!' Instead, she froze, not stopping him as he picked up the paper and immediately frowned a lot more.

He set it down and said calmly, 'OK. I'm going to have a shower.'

Amy felt totally confused. What kind of a reaction was that? Shouldn't he be denying it? Or begging for forgiveness? It didn't make any sense.

'Damien?' She gripped his arm as he walked near her, but he shook it off, which made her blood run cold.

He didn't look at her, either. 'Amy, I'll talk to you afterwards, OK? Right now I'm . . . well, I'm trying not to get annoyed with you for getting hysterical about that pack of lies.'

Amy wanted to wail, 'I'm not hysterical!' but she was saved by a knock at the cottage door. Was it time for Damien's counselling session? Amy hadn't even had a chance to tell Damien about talking to Josh this morning.

But through the patterned glass was the unmistakeably skinny and female outline of Rosay.

Damien groaned. 'Great, that's all I need. Later, OK, Ames?' He retreated into the bathroom.

She opened the door to Rosay automatically, in a total daze, thinking about Damien and what he'd said. At least from the way he'd behaved she was pretty sure he wasn't cheating on her. But she still thought he was hiding *something*. And now he was angry with her in his own stubborn Damien-like way, and maybe he had a point. She'd been unreasonable. Her stomach hurt.

'Amy! What on earth is the matter with you? Where's Damien?'

'Oh. Hi, Rosay. Nuh-nothing. He's just in the shower. Come in – oh.'

Rosay strode in and plonked herself down on the sofa,

picking up the paper that Damien had left there and tutting loudly. 'Well, what did I say? Alkie Paige Young, up to her tricks again! I must say, I didn't think it would happen this quickly.' She looked up, almost triumphant.

Amy tried not to react but tears sprang to her eyes. She didn't want to cry in front of Rosay of all people.

'Oh, Amy, you poor thing. Listen, pack your stuff and move into the house. I'll explain it to Mum. She loves you, anyway, and the guest wing's nearly finished.'

'What? No! No, I can't. Anyway, it's just gossip. Damien said –'

'What? Did he deny it? Typical man!' She lowered her voice, even though the sound of running water was now coming loudly from the bathroom. 'Marc denied it too, you know. I believed him, like some sap, until I saw the texts.' Rosay shuddered at the thought. 'Have you checked his phone?'

'But it's not – I don't think it's true. You said yourself that you can't believe a word of what's in the papers.'

Rosay hit lightly at the paper. 'Yes, but also, there's no smoke without fire. There could be a *germ* of truth in it. Is that his phone over there? Do you mind if I –?'

Amy lunged towards Damien's phone. 'No! Don't you dare!' She shook her head, horrified at the thought.

'Suit yourself.' Rosay sniffed. 'Well, I just want you to know you've got a place to stay if you need it.' She looked thoughtful. 'Or maybe you could stay here on your own. I could work on Carlo to get Damien kicked off the team and –'

'Oh my God! No!' Surely Rosay couldn't really do that? Amy felt a fierce rush of protectiveness towards Damien. 'That's just crazy.'

'Relax! It's not something that happens overnight. Even getting rid of Marc after the Paige thing was difficult.'

'But Marc Frampton was injured.'

'I know.' Rosay's lips twitched in a half-smile.

Amy forgot all the emotional turmoil she was going through and remembered her new suspicions about Rosay. Was she suggesting she had something to do with Marc's injury?

'Oh, don't worry! I didn't do anything – not physically. But there are things you can do to a player's mind, you know. Throw them off a bit. And he deserved it.'

Rosay fiddled with the delicate watch on her wrist. 'Anyway, listen, I came over to see if you needed anything and if you were ready for the spa.' She looked Amy up and down. 'But I can see you're clearly not. What happened to your hair? Have you got GHDs handy or do you want to come over and borrow mine? Maybe you should come over anyway, if Damien's going to be a long time in the shower. It must be impossible having only one bathroom – you poor thing! I've got a dressing room with an en suite – well, it's one of the spare rooms, but it's become my dressing room, you know.' She laughed.

Amy looked doubtfully in the direction of the bathroom. She should stay and talk to Damien. But as soon as she thought about it, that sinking feeling returned. She didn't understand what was going on with him and what exactly had happened between them, but maybe giving him more time would be a good thing. Damien had that session coming up with Josh – *that* thought gave her butterflies, which felt wrong – and by the time she saw him this evening they'd both have chilled out more. Though she couldn't really imagine Damien talking to Josh about her. Or about anything, really.

Then she thought of something. 'But why would I want to do my hair if I'm going to a spa? Isn't that all about steam rooms and stuff?'

Rosay shook her head. 'Amy. You're not just going to a spa. You're going to a·spa with *Claudette Harris*. Believe me, you want to look good. Plus I know there will be paps waiting for you outside the spa.' She walked towards the door and picked up the Orange County bags that Amy had left there. 'We'll need these. Now come on. There's work to do. I've only got two hours to get you ready!'

12

Amy was trying so hard to keep a smile on her face that her whole head hurt. Or maybe it was the hairstyle Rosay had given her. Each strand of her hair was pulled up separately and piled on her scalp in a seemingly haphazard way that took hours to do.

But, more likely, her head was hurting because it was the only part of her body that wasn't swathed in seaweed, bandages and what she was sure was cling film, although the assistant called it something like 'pseudo-dermo wrap'. She felt a bead of sweat form on her forehead and she couldn't even lift her arm to wipe it away. Really, this wasn't very dignified, never mind warranting a full two hours of getting ready beforehand. Amy stifled a giggle. What *must* she look like? If Asha and Susi could see her now!

And yet Claudette was sitting calmly beside her, enveloped in the same wacky treatment and acting like it was perfectly normal.

When they'd first got to the spa, Claudette had led Amy around various treatment rooms, including some that had double-seater thrones in them that Claudette said were ideal for 'when you bring Damien here'.

'Oh, this isn't his cup of tea,' Amy had told Claudette, wondering whether it was hers either. She'd never seen anything like this place. The walls and floors were all white, but the atmosphere wasn't remotely clinical. There was soft jangly music playing and an exotic incense-like scent in the air. Amy was shown mud treatment rooms, flotation tanks and stone detox treatment rooms, each more unusual than the last. Then there were tanning rooms and treatment rooms, which Amy peered into through tiny windows, seeing women reclining in complicated chairs as if they were at the dentist. They looked about as cheerful as if they were having root canal treatment, too.

'Darling, Damien doesn't get a choice. You have to bring him.' Claudette gave a dramatic sigh. She'd taken off most of her jewellery – apart from the huge diamond ring – but she moved as if she was still wearing it. 'You see, the club think they've thought of everything. Carlo di Rossi has his entourage – physios, dieticians, even a psychologist now.' She shook her head. 'But really it's the wives and girlfriends that keep the players match fit. We're the ones that really take care of the boys. Sometimes I think we should get more recognition for it. You have no idea, Amy, how incredibly important you are to Damien Taylor's success, and in turn to that of the Boroughs. Carlo di Rossi should have given *you* the transfer fee.'

Amy had thought about saying that things weren't even going that well between her and Damien right now. But she didn't really want to talk to Claudette about it.

Instead she'd said, 'Does Danny come here?' She certainly couldn't picture the Boroughs captain sitting about in a white fluffy robe having a pedicure.

'Of course he does. He knows what's good for him. He needs to relax, away from the stresses of being benched in favour of the useless Scott White.' She grimaced as she led Amy to another white room. This one had a large seat at the back, covered in white fur, and softer music playing. She sat down. 'Damien will come here too, when you tell him to. Don't forget you're the boss.'

Amy could only smile in response as the assistants came in to start the treatment.

And now here they were, wrapped in some kind of bizarre . . . *stuff*.

'You'll find this takes a good centimetre or two off your waistline, and all round, Amy,' Claudette told her, while her thin yet expressive eyebrows seemed to add '*and you need it*'. 'I always do this before an important night out.'

'Oh, where are you going tonight?' Amy asked.

'It's where we're going next week that's the point,' Claudette drawled. 'I thought we should start a regime and give our bodies a chance to work out the toxins fully. I'll expect you here again at the same time tomorrow, and every day until the big night.'

'What big night?' Amy's nose tickled as a bead of dampness hit it, and she guessed that 'working out the toxins' was a polite way of saying 'sweating like a pig'.

'The premiere, of course. We'll have facials later in the week. You definitely need twenty-four hours after their special eyebrow treatment, otherwise you can't wear make-up.' The thought made Claudette's nose wrinkle like the cling film on her leg. 'And you'll need to use the Saint Tropez tanning facilities every day, too. It's the first time you'll be properly in the limelight, reflecting the image of Damien and the team. Your first real media appearance. It's highly important.'

'Sorry, what did you say?' None of Claudette's words meant anything to Amy. In fact, what she'd said made less sense than wearing mascara when your face was dissolving into your seaweed wrap, which pretty much described her right now.

Claudette went on as if she hadn't heard her. 'And I've booked you in to see Rico, my hairdresser, next Tuesday, the big day – he'll know what's best for you. You might need some extensions. And maybe some eyelash tinting.' She finally seemed to notice Amy's expression. 'Oh, did I forget to tell you about the premiere?'

Amy nodded. 'You did.'

'Well, there's not much to say. We're going to a premiere. In Leicester Square.'

'Of a film?'

'No, of a tiddlywinks match.' Claudette snorted, but in a ladylike way. 'Yes, of a film. It's that ground-breaking romantic comedy thing they've been going on about for months. There are some big stars coming from LA. It's a fairly last-minute invitation, which means some other star has cancelled, but, honey, I'm not proud when it comes to a red-carpet photo op! And they've specifically only invited Danny and Damien from the Boroughs, which means me and you. Well, they invited Scott White, really, but I have the tickets and I'm taking the liberty of passing them on to Damien because I'm not having bleedin' *Scott White* there! They only invited him to get the pictures of Paige Young, anyway, and you're as baby-faced as her.' Claudette laughed. 'No offence, darling. Paige is right. I'm jealous of your *youth*.'

Amy frowned at the mention of Paige. Well, Claudette seemed to know about everything – she might be a good person to put Amy's mind at rest.

'Um, so did you see that gossip column today?' she asked, trying to keep her voice casual. 'The thing about Paige and Damien?'

'There was no photo evidence,' said Claudette calmly.

Amy supposed that meant 'yes'.

'I've heard that Paige is about to resurrect her singing career in some new reality TV show,' Claudette continued. 'Some trash. They even approached my PR guy about me doing it, ages ago – they asked me first, of course, before Paige. But I wouldn't touch it with a bargepole, personally. Reality TV is so *desperate*. I have more dignity.'

Amy caught herself wondering whether Paige might get locked into some kind of Big Brother house, well away from her boyfriend.

'Anyway, Paige just wants to get back into the limelight. She probably started the rumour herself. I know how the PR machine works. Don't you worry about it, baby.'

Amy wasn't sure if any of this made her feel better or not. After all, Claudette hadn't said that the rumours weren't true.

But Paige had seemed so nice. Amy was definitely starting to lose her finely tuned Stanleydale instincts about who was trustworthy and who wasn't. Claudette, for example, liked to cut everyone down to size, but her heart seemed to be in the right place. Rosay said she was a fake but maybe she was lying, like Paige had suggested.

Two assistants dressed all in white breezed into the room. 'Time to unwrap!' one of them declared, smiling.

'About time!' Claudette exclaimed. 'I've released enough toxins to pollute a small planet!'

The assistants laughed politely. They began the painstaking process of peeling off layers of cling film and seaweed.

The woman who'd been unwrapping Amy produced a tape measure from her pocket and circled Amy's waist with it.

'Almost an inch!' she declared proudly.

'What did I tell you, darling,' Claudette drawled.

They all looked at Amy expectantly. 'Uh . . . great. Thanks,' she murmured, although as a way of feeling slimmer and fitter, swimming in Rosay's pool this morning had felt a hundred times better than this.

After a quick but luxurious shower, Amy joined Claudette back in the same room, just as a different pair of white-clad assistants appeared at the door. 'Ladies, are you ready for your pedicure?'

'Oh, yes. You're in for a treat, Amy.' Claudette sat back on the fur seat.

The new assistants knelt at Amy and Claudette's feet and Amy laughed to herself at the thought that someone was worshipping her. She had her feet massaged, glad that thanks to Rosay she'd freshly painted her toenails. Then her feet were slathered in some kind of fruity-smelling cream and wrapped in odd-looking cloth slippers.

The assistants left the room and Amy was just starting to relax when Claudette said, 'I wanted to warn you about something, Amy. And make you an offer.'

'OK,' said Amy slowly, wondering what Claudette could possibly be talking about.

Claudette laughed. 'It's OK, it's nothing scary.' She lowered her voice. 'Have you been gossiping about the other players, or about any of us?'

'What? No,' Amy said defensively, feeling instantly a hundred times less relaxed. 'Why?'

'Let's see. For example . . .' Claudette sat forward and spoke in a squeaky voice. '*Claudette acts like she's better than everyone.*'

Amy felt startled. She recognized those words.

'*You* said it, Amy. To Rosay, on Saturday, and she told me today.'

Amy's stomach went hot. 'I didn't say that!' She thought about it – her first night when Rosay had listed all the WAGs and the reasons she didn't like them, and she'd asked if Amy agreed, and Amy had said yes. But was Rosay making it sound like Amy was badmouthing everyone? This was awful!

'Look, I'm sorry,' Amy said. 'Honestly, I didn't mean to say anything bad about you.'

Claudette laughed. 'It's no problem. Rosay always tells me things – she and I have an arrangement. But I'll tell you what, this time I had to wheedle it out of her!' She leant closer. 'The point is, I want you to know that I get to hear everything. All the gossip, all the rumours and secrets.'

Amy waggled her wrapped feet, feeling uncomfortable. Claudette had chosen her moment well, when she had no chance of walking out.

'Also, I have an excellent PR person,' Claudette continued. 'You'll never see a bad picture of me in any magazine. I'm glamour all the way.'

Amy nodded. She'd already noticed that.

'The thing is, I use the information I get for the greater

good. I care about the Boroughs. Every team member – well, most of them. Every team member's girlfriend or wife. You all reflect on the image of the team, and my husband's the captain, so it all reflects on me.'

Amy wondered if that was why Claudette acted ten years older than her age. She seemed to have appointed herself as some kind of mother figure for the whole team.

'You see, my PR guy is brilliant at keeping sensitive things out of the paper. I don't think he does such a good job for everyone,' Claudette said. She lowered her voice. 'The truth is, he adores me.'

'Oh,' Amy said. 'So does he block certain pictures, or something?'

'Pictures and stories, yes. Although if they're really big money – huge scandals, I mean – then it can be impossible. Oh, and it works the other way, too. He gets the positive news and the glamorous pictures of me out there.'

'I never knew you could do that.'

'Well, baby, now you know. And the offer's there for you, too. All you have to do is make sure you tell me everything you know, whatever you hear, however big or small.'

The assistants came in and started fussing around at Amy's feet as she wondered what she could possibly hear about that Claudette didn't already know.

When the treatment was over, Claudette slipped gold flip-flops on and padded out into the main building of the spa. Amy followed her in a bit of a daze to their next appointment, which was a French manicure.

Finally, after a quick health drink in the Zen relaxation room, it was time to go.

She watched Claudette at the reception desk, handing over her platinum credit card with a flourish.

Amy panicked. She'd forgotten she was going to have to pay for this! There was already so much on her dad's credit card, and she hadn't asked Rosay for that money. Also she'd tried on most of the new clothes this afternoon with Rosay, wearing a whole new outfit here at Rosay's insistence that it was perfect. Then she'd accidentally dripped some wheatgrass smoothie on it. There was no way she was going to be able to take *that* back.

She thought about the way her mother hated using plastic at all – she called it 'the never-never'. One time, when her dad had taken unpaid time off work to look after her mum, Amy had heard her mum relent and tell him, 'Don't worry. Needs must. Put it on the card and make the minimum payment. We'll catch up.'

Amy guessed they *had* caught up, too. She certainly never heard her parents talk about it again.

The receptionist handed Amy a piece of elaborate gold-edged paper with a list of all the treatments she'd had and the grand total at the bottom.

And it *was* grand.

Amy bit her lip.

'What's the matter, darling?' Claudette asked, clicking her Gucci bag shut. She had a different handbag every time Amy saw her.

'Oh, nothing,' Amy said. She wasn't about to act like a child in front of Claudette, and anyway, she had the solution. She'd put it on the card, give her dad the money to cover the minimum payment, and promise to catch up later. It wouldn't be hard to find the funds, especially once she got Rosay's share. She handed the credit card to the assistant and attempted a smile as she struggled to enter her dad's PIN without ruining her new nails.

Amy's thoughts were so full of premieres and nails and credit cards that she almost forgot to be nervous about her earlier argument with Damien until she'd said goodbye to Claudette at Caseydene.

The excitement in her stomach turned to dread as she watched Claudette's car cruise away and she realized she didn't know whether Damien was still in a mood with her. He might not even want to go to a red carpet event together. It was hardly his scene – posing and playing dress-up for the cameras.

Then she remembered he wasn't exactly Stanleydale's Damien any more. *This* Damien owned Danny Harris by Armani trousers – bought with another girl.

Amy tried to ignore the angry feelings churning round her stomach as she walked up the path to the cottage and let herself in.

Damien was slumped on the sofa pointing a remote control at a football match on the telly.

'All right?' he said gruffly when he saw her.

It wasn't friendly, but it was a start. At least he was speaking to her.

Amy perched next to him, wondering how she could feel nervous around her boyfriend after all this time.

'Hi!' she started over-brightly. 'I've been to the spa with Claudette.' She stretched out her arms to show him her beautiful nails.

It was possibly the wrong thing to do. Damien wasn't exactly into spas and French manicures.

'Oh, great,' he said, barely looking, and sounding like he meant the opposite.

'It, er, was.'

Damien coughed. 'I mean, don't mind me, will you? I only get one day off a week, if that. But you go sneaking off without even leaving me a note or sending a text – that's fine. I call you and your phone rings in one of your millions of bags over there.' He waved his hand to indicate a pile of Amy's stuff by the door. 'You left it behind *again*.'

Amy's hand flew to her mouth. 'Oh no! Sorry!' She realized he was right – he said he'd talk to her when he came out of the shower, but she'd disappeared with Rosay, and then with Claudette. And without her phone. For hours. She'd been so caught up in everything she hadn't even realized.

'That's all right,' said Damien. 'It's not like I thought you were going to dump me or anything, all because of some stupid gossip rag.'

'Damien!' She turned to face him. He wasn't joking. He looked thoroughly miserable. She ached to put her arms around him. 'You didn't really think that, did you?'

'Dunno. No.' He gave an angry shrug and he pouted like his little brother. 'Maybe.'

'Well, I'm sorry. I really am. I realize I was stupid to think twice about that stuff in the paper. Claudette's been telling me all afternoon about how gossip is all controlled by PR people and, oh, listen, she's invited us to a premiere –'

Damien stopped her. 'Amy, I don't care.'

'You don't care? About the premiere? Or the PR, and Claudette? Or do you mean the gossip?'

'Yes! All of it! I've come here to play football, not be part of some . . . gossipy freak show. I want to make a go of it. I'm serious about it. But you . . . you've only been here five minutes and you're already acting all weird . . .'

'I'm not acting weird!'

He looked straight at her. 'So why didn't you tell me you'd lost the necklace I gave you?'

Amy touched her bare neck. 'What? I've barely seen you to tell you *anything*!' Then a terrible thought popped into her head. 'Did you notice that yourself? That I wasn't wearing your necklace, I mean?' She narrowed her eyes. 'Or did Paige tell you?'

Damien folded his arms. 'I saw it in the paper. It wasn't there, on your picture.'

'Oh.' Amy felt ashamed of herself for thinking the worst. She picked up the paper that was still lying on the sofa.

'But you can barely see my neck in this!'

Damien shrugged. 'Well, OK, Paige also mentioned it yesterday.'

Why hadn't he said that *first*? Amy couldn't stop herself. 'So you only noticed because Paige told you about it! You see her more than you see me!'

'Here we go again! And you tell me you're not acting weird!'

'I'm not! *You* are!'

'Listen to yourself. You have got to stop saying these ridiculous things about Paige!'

'And you have got to stop –' Amy managed to stop herself

from finishing that sentence. She was going to say 'seeing Paige'. Even she had to admit that it sounded a bit extreme. 'Stop thinking I'm acting weird,' she said.

There was a long silence where they glared at each other.

Then Damien sighed and said, 'OK, you're right. Come here.'

She scooted closer and he took her in his arms. 'I'm sorry,' he said.

'I'm sorry too,' she said.

He smiled. 'I'm *really* sorry.'

'I'm really sorry, too.'

It was what they always did after a row.

'Then we're even.' He leant towards her and she couldn't resist kissing him.

They kissed for a while, and then Damien said, 'But I can't believe you didn't take better care of that necklace. That was my heart you lost, remember.'

Amy shifted away from him, indignant. 'I didn't do it on purpose! I was really upset about it!'

'So upset you didn't even tell me?'

'Damien, we've been through this!'

He smirked. 'I know, I know. Kidding. Get back here, Ames.'

So she did. They usually had a fight over something stupid every few months, and it was almost worth it because making up with Damien was always brilliant.

On the other hand, it was worrying that she'd needed to make up with him more than once, in less than a week.

13

In the next few days, Amy settled into a strange routine. She wasn't sure whether she loved it or hated it.

She loved the freedom and the luxury she was getting used to, with the swimming and the spa and the huge baskets of healthy food that Eva brought over at regular intervals, together with any post and a paper. The mail was particularly fab. For the last couple of days, along with the cute cat postcards from her mum, she'd been receiving parcels that turned out to contain expensive make-up and beauty products, elaborately presented and accompanied by letters going on about how perfect they were for her.

She hated the way she hardly ever saw Damien, and when she did, he was tired and snappy and didn't really have time for her. He bought her presents to make up for it, items he hurriedly bought from the jeweller's close to the Royal Boroughs training ground, including a gold bracelet that was supposed to replace the lost necklace. But Amy would rather spend time with him instead.

Every day, she'd wake up to an empty house, because Damien's training started early, even for her. So she'd get up and go for a leisurely swim in Caseydene's gorgeous pool.

Josh would turn up somewhere in the middle of her swim and she'd watch him practise his serve for a while before joining him at the tables. He started bringing flasks of coffee and she brought health bars and low-calorie snacks from the food baskets.

Josh said Big Carl never needed him until the afternoon, so they would sit for ages, sharing their food and drink and chatting about everything and nothing. Josh didn't mention his sessions with Damien and Amy didn't like to ask, though she was curious. Damien hadn't said a thing about it.

After her coffee break, she'd leave Josh at the tennis courts and wander over to the main house to help Barbie with the Boroughs' start-of-season party. She spent an hour or so every day in a small room that Barbie called 'the office', ringing florists, stationers and department stores, asking for catalogues and getting quotes. It was a lot of fun, especially after Barbie decided that Amy could use the di Rossi platinum card on an unlimited budget. Eventually, Amy settled on the most expensive tablecloths and contrasting napkins she'd found because they were the nicest, but it still felt odd paying so much for them.

Around noon, Rosay would groaningly get up to eat her breakfast – or rather, drink her breakfast of black coffee. When Amy heard her stumbling to the kitchen, she'd stop party planning and join her. Amy had quickly forgiven her for telling Claudette what she'd supposedly said, after Rosay pleaded that Claudette had tricked her into it. Amy could definitely imagine that.

They'd examine the day's papers together and look at blogs and websites to see whether any Boroughs players or girlfriends were pictured in them, and if so what they were wearing and what the latest rumours were.

Rosay seemed to know exactly where to look. She pulled up a load of gossip sites Amy had never heard of, including one called *GossMonger.com*, which was running a 'WAGs Special' and encouraging anyone and everyone to contribute amateur snaps. Amy spotted a few grainy, out-of-focus shots of herself in the cringe-worthy outfits she'd worn in her first couple of days in London.

Then there were the magazines – Amy's fashion mistakes had already made it firmly into the 'NOT' side of a couple of 'HOT OR NOT?' columns, and *All Talk* magazine described her clothes as 'fashion oh-my-god-don'ts', saying things like '*Amy is pictured here wearing animal prints that quite literally went out with the ark*'.

But as the days went on, the pictures of Amy were fewer and more flattering. There was even a piece in the ultra-stylish *Gabriella* magazine that contained a verdict from an ex-assistant to Karl Lagerfeld in his Chanel days. The man praised Amy's last few outfits as 'a masterclass in street-influenced edgy elegance'. She had laughed at that – it appeared that Primark really were on the pulse of popular fashion provided you mixed it with a bit of designer gear. After reading this, Rosay finally announced that Amy really didn't have to worry any more, and so she tried not to.

Amy's fashion about-turn was partly due to all the time she spent in Rosay's dressing room. Rosay had an extra double bedroom, with en suite bathroom, that was entirely for her clothes, and after her breakfast she and Amy would go up there and try out new looks or do each other's hair and make-up, with Rosay's iPod blaring louder than Barbie on a good day.

Rosay wasn't like Asha and Susi, but Amy thought she was becoming a real friend, especially because she was great at sympathizing with Amy's loneliness and her practically invisible boyfriend. She told Amy she'd felt the same with Marc, sometimes, and said she should concentrate on being happy in herself. Her tips for achieving this – wearing a certain new expensive perfume or changing the way she did her eyeliner, for example – were a bit different from Amy's ideas of doing extra swimming and ringing Asha and Susi more often. But Amy still appreciated the effort Rosay was making to cheer her up.

In return, Amy listened to Rosay moaning about all the other girls. Amy no longer felt irritated by the way she did this – it was obvious now that Rosay felt inferior to them and needed a boost. So Amy made sure she told her as often as possible that she was as good as the others, as glamorous and as beautiful as them, and she shouldn't be scared. It helped Amy herself to feel less intimidated, and Rosay seemed to lap it up. 'Do you really think so?' she'd keep saying, and Amy would wonder yet again why someone who lived a life like Rosay's seemed to need so much reassurance.

After a couple of hours of all this, it was time for Amy to go to the spa with Claudette. Amy would undergo whatever facials and massages and tanning and general top-to-toe treatments Claudette had planned. She was starting to look forward to it every day.

But the best bit came straight afterwards. That was when Amy went shopping. If Claudette wanted to go with her, they'd go to the smart boutiques on New Bond Street. The staff always recognized them and made special recommendations, offering discounts and freebies galore.

Mostly, though, Claudette would announce mysteriously that she had other things to do, and she'd leave Amy to wander around like a proper Londoner. Amy got increasingly relaxed about the baseball cap and shades, only wearing them if she thought they added to her look. After all, she was fast becoming a total style princess and she had nothing to hide.

She usually headed for the massive Topshop in Oxford Street, or the large high street stores that surrounded it. At least she could buy the odd thing there and be her almost-normal self. She'd had a few repeats of Sunday's experience with Damien, with girls staring at her and making jealous-sounding comments about Damien's hotness, or just giggling a lot, and paparazzi snapping at her heels and calling out rude things. But Amy was getting used to it now, and she took it in her stride. She found herself walking differently – her head held high, almost daring someone to recognize her. Sometimes she even stopped and posed for the cameras, or she smiled and said hello to the giggling girls, which seemed to make them clam up altogether.

Choosing clothes on her own felt weird at first, but Amy quickly started to love it. No one could tell her what did and didn't suit her, or whether anything seemed bad quality or overpriced – she was completely her own person, which felt fantastic, and made the magazine praise even sweeter. Of course, even with the boutique freebies and the bargain high-street purchases, Amy knew she was probably spending quite a bit of money. But the credit card in her handbag was starting to feel the same as Barbie's – unlimited and worry-free. And every day it felt slightly easier to use.

After shopping, Amy would swing her carrier bags into the car that Claudette had arranged for her to use, and a driver would whisk her home to spend the rest of the afternoon and evening listening out for the sound of a key in the door. She didn't like to admit to herself that she was waiting for Damien, so she'd fill up her time trying on clothes and tidying the already immaculate cottage, unless Susi or Asha were off work, in which case she could chat to them for ages. She rang her parents a few times, too, but it was a strain having to pretend to them that everything was going perfectly, and she didn't want to mention the shopping, either, not until she had the money from Rosay for the credit-card bill.

A few nights Damien got in at eight, exhausted and wanting to veg in front of the television. The other nights he was much later, and she'd be half asleep before she heard him come in. 'Sorry, another night out with the boys,' he'd say. 'Big Carl's orders. I'll make it up to you, I promise.'

He blamed every late night on his manager, and if she said anything, he'd explain that he needed to do what was best for his game, and that included socializing with team members. 'I'm taking it seriously, Ames,' he kept saying, as if *she* wasn't. But she was making so much effort to fit in here and say the right things to Claudette and wear at least two different outfits every day, on Rosay's orders, that she was sure her life was as tiring as Damien's right now. So much for a holiday.

Instead of having a go at him and asking whether there were any girls on his nights out and why she couldn't go too, she ended up ranting at Asha and Susi, and they nagged her to confront him about it.

'I don't get it, Amy,' Susi said. 'Just ask him if you can go. Or find out where he goes and turn up there. It's a free country. This isn't like you.'

'But *he's* not being like *him*,' Amy protested. 'He's so touchy now, and so serious. Plus he's always in bars and clubs, so I can't just turn up there unless it's a private party or something. The papers would have a field day if they thought I was drinking underage. You should see the stuff they print about Paige Young's drinking problem.'

'OK, but I still don't see why you're just letting him get away with this,' Susi persisted.

'I'm trying, OK! I just don't want another argument with him,' Amy snapped. 'Can we talk about something else now?'

Amy sighed, angry with herself for getting upset with her friends. It was true that she didn't want another argument with Damien. But if the summer carried on like this she knew that one was ready to explode at any minute, whether she wanted it or not.

14

It was the second Sunday of Amy's stay in London, and it should have been Damien's day off. The night before had been another late one – without her again – and he slept in most of the morning. She knew he was wiped out, but a small Susi-like voice in her head was telling her that he might be less tired if he stopped going out on nights when he had to get up early for training.

She was just about to give up on him and go for a swim when he surfaced, looking rumpled and wonderful and smiling at her. 'Ames, hiya, sorry I overslept! I can't believe we've got the day together at last!'

'Neither can I,' Amy said warily. In fact, she'd have to see it to believe it.

'I've got so many plans for things we can do! I've made a booking for something right special to start with – a surprise, OK? And then . . .'

Damien's enthusiasm was catching. Amy found herself smiling as she listened to him reeling off names of places and sights he wanted to see.

'Plus anywhere else you want to go. I don't even mind going shopping, if that's what you want, Ames.' He grinned, looking at his watch. 'Wow, it's late! We'd better get going!'

Both of them quickly had showers and got dressed. Amy threw on a fabulous new Chloé dress that Claudette had given her, insisting it wasn't her colour after all once she'd bought it. She grabbed her H&M sandals, which matched perfectly, and looked on enviously as Damien slung on some Diesel jeans and a cotton shirt she knew he'd had for ages. She liked all this dressing up but sometimes it would be nice to wear her tracksuit outside the gates of Caseydene. Either way, Damien looked totally gorgeous and she gave him a quick kiss.

'You look amazing,' he said, making her blush like one of his adoring fans.

Just as they were ready to leave the landline phone started ringing and Damien leant over to answer it.

Amy sighed. Her friends and family – and Damien's too, as far as she knew – didn't use this number. They called each other's mobiles. This had to be someone like Big Carl, announcing extra training and cancelling their day again.

But for once it didn't sound like that. 'Sure. Yeah, she's here,' Damien said. He handed the receiver over to Amy.

'Who is it?' Amy mouthed.

Damien shrugged.

She spoke into the phone. 'Hello?'

'Is that Amy?'

'Yes.'

'Amy Thornton?'

'Yes.'

'Oh, great! Hi, Amy! I'm so glad I found the right number

for you. I'm calling from *Just Gossip*.' The voice was young, female and hurried. 'Have you got time for a quick chat? Just a couple of questions. Shouldn't take more than a minute, I promise.'

'Uh . . . OK, I suppose.' Amy looked at Damien, who was playing imaginary keepie-uppie by the door. *Just Gossip* was a bestselling magazine, so what harm could it do?

'Wonderful! OK, Amy, we're doing a short piece on footballers' girlfriends and I'm just checking some facts here, for my boss, you know.' She sounded brisk. 'Can I check how old you are? Sixteen, right? And could you spell your name for me, just so I can make sure we've got it right?'

Amy told her, feeling slightly worried. She wondered if Claudette would have talked to the press so readily. Then again, the woman wasn't exactly asking her anything controversial.

'Brilliant! Thanks very much! That's all I needed to know.' There was a clicking sound, as if she was putting her pen away, and her tone changed to a friendly, chatty one. 'So how are you settling in, then? You enjoying it?'

'Yeah, it's OK,' Amy said.

'Great! Ooh, hey, I bet you've met some of the other footballers' wives and girlfriends now, haven't you?'

'Yes.'

'Wow, really? All of them?'

'Most of the Boroughs ones, I think.'

'Wow, lucky you, that must be amazing. So, hey, what's Paige Young really like? I've always wondered, you know! She seems a bit, you know, full of herself?'

'She's . . . OK.'

'Mmm, if you say so. But you must've got a shock when

you saw the gossip about her and Damien, though. Poor you! How did you feel about that?'

Amy hesitated. She thought that gossip had blown over.

The woman laughed, filling the silence. 'I don't know – I don't think Paige is that good a singer, and you're way better-looking than her anyway, don't you think? She's a bit, you know, *fake*, and you're a natural beauty, wouldn't you say, Amy?'

Amy bit her lip. This was no longer the casual chat the reporter was making it out to be.

Damien was staring at his watch now and fiddling with the door handle, so at least Amy didn't have to lie.

'Look, I'm sorry, I've got to go.'

The girl's voice grew frostier. 'Oh, fine. Well, it's been nice chatting to you, Amy. You're a lot friendlier than Paige Young, anyway!' She laughed over-brightly. 'Or is she chattier once she's had a few drinks?'

'Sorry. Bye.' Amy hung up quickly, surprised to find her heart was pounding.

'Who was that?' Damien asked as he led her out of the door and through the Caseydene courtyard to the Mercedes.

'Someone from *Just Gossip* magazine. You know, that one Susi and Asha are addicted to?'

Damien gave her a disapproving look. 'We're not supposed to talk to reporters,' he said.

'Oh, great,' she said sarcastically. She still felt shaky from the phone call. 'Perfect. Well, it would have helped if you'd bothered to find out who was calling before you handed me the phone.'

Damien didn't reply. He opened the car door and ushered her inside.

'What was I supposed to do, anyway?' Amy carried on. 'I was already talking to her, thanks to you.'

He waited until they were settled in the car before he said, tight-lipped, 'You should have just referred her to our press officer. She handles all –'

'Wait. *We've* got a press officer?'

'Well, yeah. I mean, *I* have. But she's been fielding enquiries for you, too, since you got here. Like requests for interviews and events, you know. She keeps asking me to ask you, but –'

'But you haven't told me any of this!'

Damien shrugged. 'No, well, I was going to at some point, but I didn't think you'd be all that interested. You're here for a holiday, aren't you? Paige says this stuff is work. She turns down almost everything she's offered these days as it's too much hassle.'

The car stopped at a red light, next to a huge billboard of Paige Young in a bikini, holding a glass of a new sugar-free diet drink.

Amy nudged her head towards it. 'Yeah, I can see that. Anyway, Damien, didn't you think I needed to know this? At least about not talking to the reporters? What if I'd said the wrong thing?'

'I know you can handle yourself, Ames.'

Amy glared at him. 'Yeah, well, I can. No thanks to you.'

Damien shifted closer to her. 'Amy, come on, don't be like this. It's our special day together. Forget that stupid phone call. Just wait till you see what I've got planned!'

Amy felt herself calm down as he put his arm around her. 'It would be nice to be told things, that's all.' She leant over to wind the window down and get some fresh air.

He murmured into her hair. 'I know. I'm sorry.'

As he kissed her, a car drew level with theirs. Someone hung out of the window and a telescopic camera lens zoomed towards them through the open window.

Amy pulled away, startled, as Damien quickly wound up the window. But she didn't really feel annoyed about it. At least now the gossip columns would have evidence that she and Damien were still together.

Even so, she waited for the lights to change before she kissed him again.

This time they were interrupted by Damien's mobile ringing. Her heart sank as she listened to his brief and serious-sounding conversation, which could only be with Big Carl.

And it was exactly what she'd been dreading.

'You've been called in for extra training?' she said flatly as he hung up.

He nodded. 'Don't look at me like that! I don't like it either.' He squeezed her hand. 'But what can I do? And it's not the end of the world. We've still got a couple of hours, enough time for the surprise. And Big Carl says I need Monday off again to rest, so we can do the other stuff tomorrow, OK?'

'OK.' Amy sighed.

After a while, the car pulled up by a patch of grass near the London Eye. Amy had seen the giant big wheel on television loads of times, but it looked somehow bigger and more exciting in real life. Its glass caught the sunlight and twinkled in the distance, while colourful crowds of people filled the riverside pavement at its base.

'Is this the surprise?' Amy shifted to the edge of her seat. 'Are we going up there?'

Damien nodded, craning his neck as they got out of the car. 'Wait till you hear this! I've hired a whole capsule thingie to ourselves, and it's called a champagne flight, with drinks and chocolate truffles and stuff. Plus we won't have to queue. How cool is that?'

He smiled at her proudly and she pushed aside the thought that this was probably another one of Paige's suggestions. What did it matter? It sounded amazing, and Damien was here with *her*.

Two young girls with caked-on make-up popped up next to Amy, and one of them shoved a purple phone towards her hand. 'Can you take a photo of us with him?' she asked. The girl played with her hair and smiled confidently. 'He's really fit. I want to marry a footballer when I grow up.'

The other girl gazed silently at Damien, awestruck.

'Er . . .' said Amy.

'Look, I'm sorry,' Damien said, smiling kindly. 'We're in a rush. Bye, girls, it was nice to meet you.' He walked away.

As Amy started following him, she overheard the girl say to her quiet friend, 'Omigod! Wish I'd got a photo for your blog! Everyone at school's going to *die* when they hear we met Scott White.'

Amy slowed down a bit.

The friend seemed to get her voice back. 'That was Damien Taylor, you doughnut!' Amy heard her say. 'They look nothing like each other, apart from both being well hot!'

'You said it was that footballer that was going out with Paige Young.'

'Yeah, exactly. Damien Taylor. Keep up!'

Amy frowned and hurried after Damien, who was now

waiting patiently for her at the foot of the London Eye, ignoring funny looks from passers-by and the whispers building around him.

'That girl thought you were going out with Paige Young,' she told Damien as casually as she could manage.

He nodded into the distance. 'Yeah, well, the woman over there just asked me if I was "that one off *Hollyoaks*".' He laughed. 'Come on, Ames, let's hide away in our own private pod. I can't wait!'

It was a relief to glide upwards and away from the crowds in their own glass bubble. They had a guide with them – or 'host', as he called himself – but the man was very professional. He talked enthusiastically about being 135 metres above the ground and seeing Windsor Castle on a clear day, and he politely ignored Amy and Damien as they kissed in the warm sunlight and Amy sneaked sips of champagne.

The whole thing would have been perfect if it wasn't just about the only quality time they'd managed to spend together in a week. But for the moment it *was* their time, and the whole world of photographers, gossip and football training felt a million miles away as they circled high over London.

15

Unsurprisingly, there was no sign of Damien that night, or at least not before Amy went to bed at 2 a.m.

When she got up the next day, there was another scrawled note on the table: 'Sorry about yesterday. Will make up for it today!!! xxx'.

Amy killed time in the cottage, eating bananas from the food basket and waiting for Damien to wake up. Again. It was starting to feel like a bad habit.

At around eleven, which was three hours later than her usual swim time and an hour longer than she'd waited yesterday, she decided Damien had missed his chance. She stomped over to use the pool.

Josh was on his way out as she arrived, looking gorgeous in his clean white shorts and T-shirt, his tanned face glowing in contrast. There was a tiny bead of sweat on his forehead, giving just a hint that he'd been exerting himself.

Amy realized she was staring at him. She looked away.

He beamed a smile at her. 'You're late! And I didn't see you yesterday.'

'Damien's day off,' she mumbled. 'But then he had to go to training, so he's having extra time off today.'

He nodded. 'I'm seeing him later this afternoon.'

'Again? *Today?*' She felt like stamping on the ground and throwing things.

'Sorry, Big Carl's orders. You sound angry.'

She was in no mood to make jokes about his counselling skills. 'I need a swim.'

He gave a sympathetic shrug. 'OK, Amy. See you later.'

'Yeah, whatever,' she said as he left. She wondered why she felt so annoyed with Josh. After all, he was just doing his job. And she wouldn't even be here if it hadn't been for Josh – or more likely, Josh's dad – convincing Big Carl that footballers' personal relationships were important.

It was Big Carl she should be angry with, really, but she didn't think she had the guts to say anything to him, not when she knew how he felt about his players' girlfriends. Once, when she'd been in the office busy using Barbie's phone and credit card to order expensive party invitations, she'd heard him in the corridor, shouting, 'These wives and girlfriends are going to lose me matches!'

But she was also angry with Damien. She swam fiercely up and down the Caseydene pool, thinking about how she'd cancelled her spa sessions and her party planning for two days in a row now, all for nothing. She should just do what she wanted to, whenever she wanted. After all, Damien always did. Surely not every single one of those nights out – without her – were written into his contract with the Boroughs?

She showered, changed and, with only a second of hesitation, turned away from the cottage and set off towards the main house. Damien could wait. She knocked sharply at the door.

Rosay answered, still in her Calvin Klein dressing gown. 'Oh, hi!' she said, surprised, looking behind her. 'No Damien? Doesn't he have the day off?'

Amy must have given her such a thunderous look in response that Rosay tutted and said, 'Oh, I see. Come in and tell me all about it.'

'There's nothing to tell,' Amy said, following Rosay into the house and through to the enormous kitchen. 'He doesn't have time for me. That's it.'

'They're all like that,' Rosay sighed. 'I bet he's been saying he needs to go out every night to keep my step-dad happy.' She poured two large mugs of coffee and nudged one towards Amy.

'That's exactly what he's been saying.'

'Marc was the same. It's outrageous, isn't it? It's just an excuse. But still, what can we do? We have to put up with it. At least he's not cheating on you or anything. Though most of them expect you to put up with that, too.' Rosay paused and sipped her coffee. 'Has he mentioned Paige again?'

'Not much,' said Amy. 'So at least that's a good sign.'

Rosay didn't say anything.

'Isn't it a good sign?'

'Well, yes, it could be. But . . .'

'But what?'

'Well . . . it's just that if he really had nothing to hide, then maybe he would talk about her more.'

'Are you saying he has something to hide?' Amy looked at Rosay in alarm. Maybe Rosay had seen them together or something! Amy realized that she didn't really know what Rosay did in the evenings. Once or twice, she'd suggested that the two of them should go out, but Rosay had always made some excuse. And Rosay frequently moaned about not having any friends. Yet a couple of times when Amy had heard an engine late at night and peered out of the windows hoping for Damien, she'd seen the Mercedes that she and Rosay used arriving back at the mansion doors instead.

'Rosay, do you *know* something?' she asked.

'No, no,' Rosay said quickly. 'Well, there is just one thing . . .'

'What?' Amy's voice was sharper than she'd intended.

'I heard a rumour that Scott and Paige are breaking up.'

'Well, it can't be true,' said Amy. 'Paige invited me to a party at Kylie's boyfriend's house this Wednesday, and she said she was going with Scott.' Then she remembered she wasn't supposed to mention the party to Rosay. She cringed inside.

'Oh, a party,' said Rosay. 'Sounds nice.' She swirled the coffee in her cup and examined it closely.

Amy's heart sank. 'I'm sorry,' she said. 'It's all couples . . .' She realized that didn't sound much better, when Paige had split Rosay and her boyfriend up. 'I mean, they only wanted . . .' She sighed. She should be honest. 'Actually, I don't know what their problem is.'

'Don't worry,' said Rosay bitterly. 'I do.'

Amy wracked her brain for ways to make her friend feel less awful about being an outcast, and at the same time make herself feel better about putting her foot in it. She looked at the time. Two o'clock – the time she usually left to meet Claudette at the spa. And Claudette was friends with Rosay, wasn't she? Well, she said she wasn't, and she didn't behave like it in front of other people, but she popped round often enough to speak to her. Amy had seen it with her own eyes.

'Listen, I might go to the spa with Claudette now after all. Why don't you come with me?'

'I can't. Claudette doesn't want me around,' Rosay said simply. Then she shrugged, as if she really didn't care. 'Same as Kylie doesn't.'

'Kylie does want you around,' Amy lied.

'She doesn't. None of them do. I had no girls left to talk to at the Boroughs until you came along.' She sniffed. 'God, sorry, I sound pathetic. I don't know why I care when being involved becomes so bitchy anyway. They can take their secret parties and their exclusive spa sessions and leave me alone.'

'Well, I don't understand it.' Amy felt out of her depth. 'You were so lovely to me from the minute I got here . . .'

'No, I wasn't.' Rosay stared at her hands. 'But thanks for saying it, anyway.'

Amy shrugged. 'Well, I thought you were. You really helped me. You should let the others see that side of you more and maybe things wouldn't be so bad. I mean, the Boroughs girls need a referee more than the boys do!' she laughed.

Rosay smiled. 'You think? I don't know,' she said, perking up a bit. 'But there is one way I could help Kylie out . . .'

'Yeah? What is it?' Amy asked, pleased that she could at least get some relationships back on track. 'You should go for it!'

But Rosay had flopped again. 'No, it won't work. They'd probably hate me even more.'

'Well, you could try,' Amy enthused, not wanting to give up. She stared down at her now-familiar manicured nails wrapped around the coffee cup. 'Anyway, I'm sure no one hates you. Why would they?'

'Oh, it's a long story,' said Rosay. 'I'd rather not say in case you don't believe me, and then you hate me too.'

'Why wouldn't I believe you?' Amy asked, looking up in surprise.

'Because no one does. Don't worry about it. I'm surprised Claudette hasn't told you. I didn't expect you to talk to me any more after your first spa afternoon with her.'

'But Claudette comes over to see you sometimes, doesn't she? I've seen her.'

Rosay shook her head. 'That's just business.'

'I don't understand.' Amy remembered her awkward conversation with Claudette the first time she'd gone to the spa. 'Is this to do with her PR guy, and how she wants to hear all the gossip?'

'Don't you love the retro-bling on this Marc Jacobs dress?' Rosay said, pointing to a magazine cover on the kitchen counter. Amy understood that Rosay didn't want to talk about it, so she let the subject drop.

But when Rosay left minutes later to get ready for some appointment she said she had in the West End, Amy decided to go ahead with her last-minute plan of meeting Claudette after all. It was time to find out what was really going on with her new friend.

16

The spa staff were so used to seeing Amy with Claudette that they said, 'Mrs Harris is already here,' and sent her in the direction of a treatment room at the end of a long white corridor.

'Baby!' Claudette exclaimed through the thick gloop that was spread all over her face. 'I didn't expect to see you on the lads' day off. Trouble in paradise?'

'If there's going to be girl talk, should I leave?' said the person sitting next to Claudette, who had hairy legs and a face caked in similar gloop.

'Or you could simply shut up, Danny,' Claudette said.

Amy stared in surprise. Danny Harris was sitting in a treatment room having a facial with Claudette.

'Sorry to . . . interrupt,' Amy said.

'Oh, you're not interrupting,' Claudette said. 'There's room for one more.' She patted the bench next to her. 'Anyway, I'm glad you're here. I nearly called you and Damien in. It's your last chance to cleanse thoroughly before tomorrow's premiere. Both of you.'

'Oh, right,' said Amy, wondering whether Damien would even remember the premiere, let alone be willing to come to a spa with her to 'cleanse' for it.

Danny stood up. 'Nothing personal, Amy, sorry, but I think I *will* leave. This stuff is burning my skin. I'm going to find someone to remove it.'

'Danny Harris, stop being such a wuss!' Claudette called.

He left anyway, wiggling his fingers at her behind his back.

'Sit, Amy,' said Claudette, sighing.

Amy sat.

'Sorry about him. Now why are you really here? More suspicions about Paige and your boyfriend?'

Why did everyone keep mentioning that? Amy's heart pounded. 'Why, what have you heard?'

'Nothing, darling! Well, maybe a little something about Scott . . . Don't look so scared. Has that Rosay been up to her tricks again, stirring things up?'

'Well . . .' said Amy. 'Actually, it's Rosay I sort of wanted to speak to you about.'

'What's she done now?' Claudette laughed. 'Is it about the pap shots? Do you want to speak to my PR guy about it? We can set up a proper shoot for you and Damien. It might get them off your back for a bit, even with Rosay's best efforts.'

Amy frowned. 'What are you talking about?'

Claudette's face mask stretched in disbelief. 'You're not seriously telling me you hadn't guessed?'

'Guessed what?'

'About Rosay's hotline to the paps, of course. The way she sells out all her friends on a regular basis. Well, her ex-friends. She's out and about every day and most nights, stalking us and telling the paps where we are. Luckily Danny and I have the PR guy to protect us. I barely notice her.'

'She spies on you?' said Amy.

'And on you. I thought it was obvious, darling.' Claudette laughed. 'She gives the paps tip-offs. Low, isn't it? She's like a leech, but we have to put up with it, with her parents being who they are.'

'But why would Rosay do something like that?'

'Oh, it's simple. Even a *baby* could understand it.'

Amy gritted her teeth and waited.

Claudette waved one hand dismissively. 'Money, of course.'

That didn't make sense. 'But why?'

'You mean, why does Rosay need the money?'

'Yes.'

'Even simpler. The reason is Paige Young – or at least, that's how Rosay sees it. Rosay blames Paige Young for everything. She seems to forget all about the crime everyone's certain she committed.'

'Crime?'

Claudette laughed and said, 'You really haven't worked *any* of this out, have you?'

'Er, no,' Amy admitted. This sounded even more complicated than she'd first thought. Why couldn't things just be normal?

'Well, good. I always love an opportunity to tell this story.' She took a deep breath. 'Darling, everyone's convinced it was Rosay, not Trina Santos, who slashed Paige's clothes to pieces last year!'

She paused, as if checking that Amy was suitably shocked before she continued.

'She had a blazing row with Paige in front of all of us just before it happened, accusing her of seeing her man. Marc Frampton, d'you remember him, darling? Well, why would

135

you – he wasn't exactly a looker, if you know what I mean.'
Claudette screwed her face up as if to illustrate his lack of
looks, though even with that and the gloopy face, she still
looked gorgeous. 'There was nothing going on between Paige
and him.'

'But how can you know that?'

'Paige wasn't Marc's type. And she was far too busy with
Trina's boyfriend, anyway. Scott White.' Claudette laughed.
'It was all a misunderstanding. But that didn't stop Rosay
from turning on Paige like a mad thing!'

'Wow,' Amy breathed. So it was Rosay who wrecked all of
Paige's things. And she hadn't let up – she still had it in for
Paige.

Plus she'd been selling out all her friends – including
Amy.

Amy's stomach sank. She felt horribly betrayed. She was
still wary of believing that what Claudette was saying was
the truth, but it did explain all the strange behaviour. She
even had good reason to believe she'd chopped up Amy's own
Chloé dress, and that was for absolutely no reason. How
could she have been so wrong about Rosay?

'Anyway, the PR guys pulled out all the stops to keep Rosay
away from the slightest suspicion. Can you imagine? It would
have been so embarrassing for Big Carl, his step-daughter
accused of petty crime like that!' Claudette's eyes, framed by
globs of white, widened in horror. 'It was pretty handy that
Paige and Scott got together so publicly and all the evidence
pointed to Trina. She made a great scapegoat because she was
about to leave for Brazil anyway. But there wasn't enough
evidence to convict Trina, and the police weren't particularly

interested in the case. It was the press who cared, and they got what they wanted.'

'But that's not fair on Trina!'

'Don't worry, Amy sweetheart.' Claudette laughed. 'You wouldn't feel sorry for Trina if you knew her. And Rosay got *her* punishment closer to home. Her mum and step-dad cut her off. No credit cards, no money, nothing. She lost her independence, too. She used to share a flat with Paige and Trina – that's when she wasn't in the cottage with fugly Marc, of course. Now she's back at Caseydene. She has a roof over her head, but her mum drives her crazy. And she has to earn her own money.'

Claudette made a face as if that was the most terrible thing in the world.

'I'll tell you, she's struggling to cope – without the clothes, the shoes, the spas, the lifestyle. She's so . . . *pale* now! The only person who'll give her a job – well, a job she's willing to do – is her own father, and even *he's* only doing it to get at her mother for eloping with the Boroughs manager. Poor Rosay.'

Amy didn't think she felt sorry for Rosay at all any more.

Claudette gave an angelic smile. 'And sometimes I put work her way – tell her where we'll be if I think the paps can get a particularly flattering shot of one of us, or if I've heard some celebrity scandal on the grapevine, as long as it doesn't affect the Boroughs.'

Amy thought she'd heard enough. But she couldn't resist asking, 'But why would you help her out?'

'Oh, because I'm a saint,' Claudette said, clasping her hands together seriously. Then she laughed. 'Not really! Because her dad is Matt Sands, of course.' She said this as if it should mean something to Amy.

'Who?'

'Oh, please. Come *on*. Sands owns one of the biggest picture agencies in Britain. He makes millions out of celebrity scandal. He works closely with my PR guy – sometimes. We have to keep him sweet.' Claudette smiled. 'Oh, and also because I want Rosay to tell me all the gossip in return. I need to know what's going on so I can keep some things out of the press. I care deeply about the Boroughs, you know. But Rosay stalks people and sells their secrets to the highest bidder. She doesn't care about any of us.' She touched her face. 'Now, be a darling and call an assistant to finish off this treatment for me, would you? They're being totally useless today. Thanks, Amy sweetheart.'

By the time Amy got home, her mind was reeling with what she'd heard. One thing was certain: Rosay wasn't the friend she'd thought she was.

She unlocked the door to the cottage in a daze.

Damien was there, in the same position as he had been a week before, slumped in front of the sofa with the remote control pointing at a football match. Amy felt an odd sense of déjà vu as he looked up and said bitterly, 'Oh, you decided to come back, then?'

She wished she could pluck the remote out of his hands and fast forward to the part where they apologized and made up. She'd already had enough drama for one day.

'Damien, do we have to have a fight? I'm annoyed with you, you're annoyed with me, now let's not waste the precious few seconds we have together by doing this.'

She sat down next to him and tried to smile, but the look on his face wouldn't let her.

He folded his arms. 'Amy, what's going on with you? I mean, *really* going on? Why can't you accept that this is my life now?'

She abandoned all hope of not having a row as the bile rose in her throat. 'Damien, you're talking utter –' She tried to keep her voice calm. 'I do accept that.'

He grunted.

'I'd just like to see you every now and then,' she continued. 'But you're always out, or sleeping, or a total grouch.'

'Huh,' he said, as if to illustrate her point. 'Apart from the fact that you weren't even here when I woke up – for the second time! Apart from the fact that there's no point even *trying* to ring you because you never answer. Apart from that, I'm always *working*, Amy. This is my job, you know. Even the socializing. I've told you a hundred times. I can't believe you don't understand!'

Amy's anger swelled. 'So I'm just supposed to sit around here waiting for you to wake up? Why don't you ask me to go with you on your nights out sometimes? I bet you could. You said yourself Paige was there last week –'

Damien pressed hard on the remote control. The football replay he was watching froze in mid-kick. 'Of course, *this* is what it's all about, isn't it?' He pressed a button to start the replay again. 'What *is* your problem with Paige? Why *shouldn't* I see her on some of my nights out?'

Amy stared at him.

So he barely saw his girlfriend, but he didn't see anything wrong with seeing Paige on his nights out?

Oddly, instead of making her angrier, it made Amy feel like all the air had been let out of her tyres. She didn't want to be right about Paige. She wanted it all to be a horrible misunderstanding, like the one about Paige and Marc Frampton. Only without the clothes-slashing and the ex-flatmates hating each other for evermore.

Damien was still ranting. 'I'm just living my life, Amy! I'm doing the best I can! Why can't you let me?'

'Oh, OK,' said Amy quietly. 'Well, yeah. Don't let me stop you.' She turned her head away because her eyes were filling with tears.

Then Damien said, 'Amy, maybe we should . . . maybe we shouldn't . . .'

He furiously pressed pause and play on the DVD player, over and over again. A footballer on the screen scored a goal in slow motion, frame by frame.

Amy gripped his arm to stop him. Her voice trembled. 'Damien, what are you trying to say?'

He stared at the telly.

'Do you want me to . . . go home?'

She held her breath.

'No,' he said softly, still staring at the telly. 'I don't. I've been dying for you to get here. I want you here.'

Amy breathed out.

'Even if you're being weird.'

She swatted his arm half-heartedly, waiting for the apology. But he didn't smile.

'Listen . . . I overheard Rosay last week, you know, when we were having that row and she came over. I was about to start the shower, and I heard her say you could go and . . . live over there, in the main house . . . and . . .'

Amy let go of his arm. 'So what are you saying? You want me to move out? When I've only been here just over a week? And it's been a crazy, crazy week?'

He started stabbing at the remote control again. 'Amy, every day is crazy here! It's been like this for me since May. I couldn't wait to see you, for some normality, but . . . it's been even crazier since you got here, to be honest. It's not working out like this. Don't you get it? I don't want to break up with you, I just need to get used to things being like this.'

'You've got a funny way of showing it,' Amy said. She was surprised by how cold her voice sounded.

Damien closed his eyes and leant his head back on the sofa. 'What I mean is, if we carry on like this we might . . . Well, it's not going to get easier. I mean it, Amy. You need to enjoy your holiday, and I need to concentrate on doing what Carlo wants me to without worrying whether you're OK with it. Maybe we both need some . . . space.'

Amy couldn't believe it. She'd never heard Damien speak like this before. The words didn't even sound like him.

'Damien, we've had nothing but space! We've had two months apart and I've barely seen you since I got here! So never mind moving in with those rich loons over there. Why don't I just go back to Stanleydale? You can't get more space than that!' She got up, stumbling slightly over the sofa leg because she couldn't see where she was going through her tear-blurred eyes.

Damien jumped up and grabbed her arm. 'Amy, please. Just try it. The training's going to get worse!' he pleaded. 'The football season starts next week. I should have thought of this before. OK, I was being selfish, wanting you here, expecting you to sit on your own all day waiting for me.'

Amy stared up at him, mascara mixed with the tears running down her face. 'I don't sit at home waiting for you!' she snapped. 'I go out and have fun, you know. I can take care of myself!'

'But you'll be less lonely, in the house, and it's just across the way! You'll have Rosay to talk to and go out with –'

Amy snorted. She knew he didn't even like Rosay, and she wasn't sure she did any more either, after what she'd heard today!

'We can still go out together. It will be more like back home, with less pressure, you know. We won't be in each other's pockets. We'll be next-door neighbours. We know *that* works.'

He gave her a small smile.

'We've got the premiere tomorrow,' she said miserably. 'Remember? And that dinner thing at Johann Haag's house on Wednesday. And that huge start-of-season party on Saturday, the one I'm helping Barbie with.'

'Exactly, yeah, that kind of thing.' Damien let out a long sigh.

Amy sat down again and stared at her perfectly manicured nails for ages. She'd never had nails like this in Stanleydale. Her hands looked different, and she felt different.

'Ames?' Damien took her hand, looked in her eyes. 'Are you OK? What do you think?'

She couldn't say what she thought, which was: does this have anything to do with Paige? Was Damien trying to get her out of the way so that he could see Paige Young – more than casually? Maybe bring her back to the cottage, or something?

It was a horrible thought.

But she was probably being ridiculous. And she already knew how annoyed he'd be if she said anything like that.

'I feel that if we have some space, we can get through this,' Damien said, sounding oddly parrot-like. 'How do you feel about that?'

Amy narrowed her eyes at him, suddenly remembering. 'I *feel* like you've seen that wannabe psychologist today.' She tried to read his expression. 'Did Josh suggest this stuff?'

Damien didn't answer, but she could tell she'd hit on something.

'What did you tell him? Do you talk about me?' And to think she was always so careful not to talk about Damien, because she was worried about treading on his toes!

'His job is to get me playing at my best, you know. It's nothing personal.'

'So you *did* talk about me?'

'Sort of.' Damien shrugged. 'He mentioned that he'd met you and you seemed down.'

She'd kill Josh! 'Down? He said I was down? He had no right to say that!' And she wasn't *down*! Well, maybe she'd been a bit moody today. But that was because she missed Damien!

'Amy, he was just making small-talk or something. But I'll tell you what. I didn't even know you'd been chatting to Josh every day. You never mentioned it to me. I felt like an idiot.'

'Didn't I?' Amy realized it was true. Then she nearly laughed. 'Wait a minute – you're not jealous, are you?'

'Course not, I'm just saying you never tell me anything any more.' Then Damien's eyes darkened. '*Should* I be jealous?'

'No, no,' Amy said quickly. Although why would he care, if he was breaking up with her? Oh, sorry – wanting *space*.

'Right. Good. Well, no, it made me think I haven't been fair to you.'

'You haven't.'

He sighed. 'You know, Ames, I didn't really want to talk to that psychologist guy, but now I'm glad I do. It sort of helps with all the craziness, in a funny way. I hope we've sorted this out, and with a bit of space I think it will all work out.'

Well, Amy thought, maybe *she* should talk to Josh again, too. And when she did, she would ask him just what he thought he was playing at.

17

Damien said he had another team night planned and Amy didn't try to stop him, or ask whether there would be any girls there, or ask to go with him, even though she wanted to say all those things.

She kissed him before he left, though.

'Ames,' he murmured into her hair. 'We'll work this out, I promise.'

Amy didn't say anything. She held him tight, then she let him go and tried not to cry.

After sitting like a zombie for a while, she packed her stuff and dragged her stupid suitcase across to the side entrance of the house. Damien told her he'd cleared it all with Barbie and Big Carl and they were expecting her. Apparently Big Carl had said he approved of the new arrangement 'as a manager, and as a father', which was highly cringeworthy. And Barbie was very excited because one of the guest rooms had just finished being decorated and she was sure Amy would love it.

Amy sighed, fearing the worst. It would probably have sequinned wallpaper or grotesque blingy curtains of some kind.

Eva let her in and showed her to her room, which was painted sugary pink, purple and white, and made her feel a bit sick. But she supposed it could have been worse. She went over to the window, which overlooked the courtyard and the cottage where Damien was now staying without her. Then she tore herself away, sat under the white lacy canopy on the four-poster bed and took out her phone, reading over all the texts Susi and Asha – and Damien – had sent her since she'd got here. She wondered what the twins would make of this when she told them. She thought she should probably tell her mum and dad, too, although they would probably approve. Her mum would say Damien was a sensible lad and they were both very young. Her dad might even be pleased, as this was the kind of living arrangement he had in mind for her London visit in the first place, with lots of potential for parental supervision.

She was about to speed-dial Asha when Rosay appeared at the door.

'Hi,' Rosay said, sounding normal and nice, and not like the clothes-slashing, pap-photo-selling maniac Claudette had been talking about. 'I heard what happened. Well, some of it. Are you OK?'

Amy shrugged and fiddled with her phone. She didn't feel like talking to Rosay – she wanted her real friends.

'Do you want to talk about it? Can I come in?' She poked her head into the pink room. 'Oh my days! What has Mum done to this room? It looks like a poodle parlour!'

Amy laughed, which Rosay took as a sign that she could bound in and sit on the bed next to her.

'I'm really sorry. Men are horrible.'

Amy felt like telling her to get out. 'Damien isn't. He just . . . wanted some . . . space.'

It still sounded ridiculous to Amy, but Rosay nodded as if it made sense. 'Yeah, sure. Don't worry – he'll come round. Hey, let's do something fun! Let's go shopping! Or raid Carlo's drinks cabinet! Or if you hate this room, we can move you into my dressing room or something! It's right next to my bedroom and we can pretend we're flatmates!'

'I'd rather stay here. Claudette told me what happened when you shared a flat with Trina and . . . Paige.' Amy didn't feel like being nice to Rosay, that was for sure. In fact, she felt positively evil.

Rosay's face fell. 'Oh. Oh, right.' She pulled a white thread from the bedspread. 'What exactly did Claudette tell you?'

'Everything.' Amy didn't even try to soften her voice.

'Oh.' She went quiet for ages. 'I was starting to think she wouldn't do that, but some hope. No one ever forgets a thing around here.'

Amy didn't say anything. After all, Rosay was just as bad. She didn't seem in any hurry to forget her issues with Paige, even though she'd more or less got away with her revenge attack.

Rosay stared out of the window. 'Anyway, you mean she told you everything according to *her*.'

Amy clutched her phone and wished Rosay would go away.

'Don't you want to hear my side of it?'

Amy shrugged. Rosay had already told her what she thought was going on between Marc Frampton and Paige, after all. What else was there to hear? Frankly she wanted this whole ridiculous world out of her mind right now. She was sick of hearing about it.

Rosay got up and walked towards the door. By the time she got there, her face had hardened. She opened the door. 'Fine. I'll leave you in peace.'

'Wait a sec.'

'Yeah?' Rosay turned back, looking hopeful.

'Are you going to pay me back for the clothes I bought on my credit card?'

Rosay frowned. 'I said I would, and I will.' Her voice was calm, but cold. 'OK? You know where to find me if you want to talk.'

Her heels clicked up the wooden corridor and faded away.

Amy lay back on the bed and wondered why being mean to Rosay hadn't made her feel better. Anyway, she deserved it. She was a stirrer and she'd caused nothing but trouble for Amy and Damien since the Saturday Amy had arrived. Plus if she hadn't gone on about Amy living in the main house, maybe Damien wouldn't even have thought of it.

She set about unpacking for the second time in two weeks, trying not to think about Damien and who he might be with right now.

The following morning, and partly to avoid seeing any of Rosay's family, Amy went to the pool even earlier than usual for the swim to end all swims.

She did fifty lengths and then ten more and she would have carried on if she hadn't seen the main door open and the unmistakeable outline of Josh coming into the building.

Her heart raced as she towelled herself off and headed for a confrontation with the lad who'd made her boyfriend think they 'needed space' when she'd just arrived to spend the summer with him. But Josh threw her immediately by taking his shirt off just as she burst on to the tennis court.

'Hi, Amy!'

He beamed a huge smile and she didn't know where to look. His amazing eyes and super-toned upper body were getting in the way of her anger.

'Hold on, I was just . . . too hot.'

She could see that, too.

He pulled a different polo shirt on, which still didn't really help because it was well-fitted and his arm muscles were straining at its sleeves. Amy decided to focus elsewhere.

'I want to talk to you,' she told his tennis racquet.

'Sure, OK. I brought coffee in case you were here today – let's find our table and I can practise later.'

'Just here is fine. What did you tell Damien about me?'

He shifted a little and then turned his sincere blue eyes on her. 'I can't discuss that with you, Amy. It's one of the first things they teach all psychologists. Conf–'

'Confidentiality,' Amy finished for him. 'Yeah, yeah. Well, he's suddenly got these ideas in his head about us needing space and I've moved into the house and –'

'Oh, I see.' He gave her a look of pure concern. 'I'm sorry. Do you want to talk about it?'

He was doing it again – making her feel special, like he had time for her and no one else. She knew that wasn't true – it was a psychologist's trick that he'd probably learnt from his parents. 'I, er . . .'

'Look, why don't we have a proper talk about this, over lunch or something? We could maybe go out somewhere for a change?' He idly served a ball over the net, then he smiled at her.

Amy's knees felt suddenly weak, which she knew was completely ridiculous. She steeled herself. 'No, I'm busy today.'

She was, too. Claudette had booked her an appointment with Rico the hairdresser, who ran a very exclusive salon in Kensington. She was planning on going shopping beforehand for a dress to wear for the premiere. It somehow felt more crucial to get it exactly right, now that it was a significant date with Damien and not just a chance to prove to Claudette – and possibly the paps – that she could be as glamorous as the other footballers' girlfriends.

'Aw, that's a shame.' Josh picked up another ball and sent it flying with considerable force. 'How about tomorrow, then?'

Before Amy could come up with a believable excuse he'd named a time and a place. Amy told herself it was his persuasive psychological powers and nothing to do with the way his muscles rippled that made her agree to meet him. After all, it wasn't a date or anything. He just felt sorry for her, and he was certainly good at cheering her up.

She set out for the shops with only a slight twinge of nerves. She'd meant to check some credit-card details last week, like how much the minimum payment was likely to be and exactly how much she'd spent so far. But her head had been so full of Damien and clothes and spas and fitting in with her new friends that she just hadn't had a chance.

Tonight was an important night. She decided to go for it and worry about it later. It was nice to be frivolous for once in her life.

It took her three high-street stores and six boutiques to settle on an Oscar de la Renta dress that was at once glamorous and understated. It was green satin with intricate floral embroidery and a flattering line – first straight, then layering outwards in ruffles until it flared over her knees. No one could possibly complain about this dress, she thought as she selected patent leather sandals and a satin bag to complement it. It didn't look like she was trying too hard – it just looked stunning. She couldn't wait till Damien saw it. Even with the shop's generous discount it was a heart-stopping amount. But if this was what it took to remind Damien of why he'd missed her so much, then it was worth it.

Then she spent well over two hours with Rico, emerging with hair that was straightened, teased, coloured, extended and sculpted to within an inch of its life. Rico's staff fussed around her and when Rico himself announced that Amy was Claudette Harris's friend, their fussing got a notch more frantic.

For once she was pleased to see the paparazzi crowded round the car door when she emerged. She knew she looked good and with designer bags swinging from her arm her confidence soared. They could print as many of these photos as they liked.

Back at Caseydene, Amy escaped to her room, exhausted. Her stomach was rumbling so she went down to the kitchen and rooted through the fridge to make herself a sandwich. It seemed like rich people had ham and cheese in their fridges too, even if it was wrapped in waxy paper instead of super-market plastic. She found a plate to put it on and she was about to take it up to her room when Barbie's loud voice made her jump.

'Oh, Amy! Amy, Amy, Amy! I need you to save my life, babe!'

Amy hesitated, balancing her plate in one hand. She could only imagine what Barbie considered to be a disaster. She turned to face her.

'You can bring your sandwich!'

Amy followed Barbie into a large oak-panelled room with an oval-shaped table in the middle. The room had an old-fashioned air about it, helped along by the fact that it was lined with bookshelves.

'The study,' Barbie explained. 'Although, babe, have to admit, I've never been one for study. Other than male behaviour, of course.' Her laugh almost shook the emptier shelves.

She pointed to a mass of white paper covering the mahogany table. 'It's the rest of it. I thought it was too much to ask, so I've had you tucked away in the box room with just a few tasks. But this is really it, all of the party-planning stuff.' She sighed. 'It's doing my head in, I swear. I need help, babe. You've done such a fantastic job on the flowers, and the tableware and stationery. I couldn't ask you to take a look at some of this too, could I? I swear I've got a migraine coming on.'

'Yes, of course,' Amy said politely. 'What do you want me to do?'

'Brilliant! If you could sort though this lot and make some calls for me? The security, the parking, the caterers, ice, drinks, the place settings, the charity rep – it all needs sorting.'

Amy had selfish thoughts about needing to get ready for her big date tonight. 'How long will that take? It sounds like a lot.'

'It is, babe, believe me.' Barbie sighed. 'The only thing I've managed is a list of guests. Oh, yeah, and Rosay said she'd sort the band. But the invitations need to be sent out urgently – do you think you could get them done before tonight?' Barbie looked at her hopefully.

'Um, I'll try.' She was grateful to Barbie for all she'd done, but it wasn't the afternoon she had planned.

'Babe, you're a superstar. Maybe you could ask Rosay to help you?'

'Yeah, maybe,' Amy said with little enthusiasm.

'Oh, I noticed you two have had a little tiff. Aw, make it up, can't you? It ain't worth it, babe – you and Rosay need each other! Friends are gold in this world! That's some free advice from your Auntie Barbie.' Some papers fluttered off the desk.

Amy picked them up. The top sheet was an order for glassware. '"Barbara-Ann di Rossi",' she read aloud. 'Oh. Is that your full name? I didn't know that.'

'Where does it say that?' Barbie snatched the paper out of her hand. 'No one calls me that. It's so *ordinary*! It's as bad as when people call my girl Rose – I mean, it might be the name on her birth certificate, but it's not very glam, is it? I've made damn sure that everyone called her Rosay, from the minute we left her dreadful father. It's French.' She crumpled the letter up. 'Honestly, I don't know about this party planner – if she can get a thing like that wrong, then maybe it's just as well she dropped us in it! We're better off without her.'

'But that piece of paper had the order for –'

'We don't need it, babe. Believe me. You can do everything from scratch. I trust you more than any party planner.'

She swept all the paper off the desk and into a nearby wastepaper bin.

'Now I've definitely got a bit of headache and I've got to look at the swatches for upstairs, so if it's all right, I'll leave you to it. I know you can do it.'

'Oh, I . . .'

'Thanks, babe. You're a true angel, you are.'

Barbie clicked out of the room.

Amy sighed. She decided she'd give it a couple of hours of her time, which still left her an hour to get ready for the premiere. She had her hair done and her dress, so how long could it take?

18

Amy raced down the Caseydene staircase, yelling goodbye to Eva and running to the gates. The car that Claudette had sent was waiting for her and probably had been for some time. She couldn't believe she was late. At least she'd managed to get all the invitations ready to be sent, and she'd get to work on the rest of it tomorrow afternoon.

Despite her nerves and her lateness, she was really looking forward to tonight. She'd had to rush her make-up, but she had her Rico hair and the new dress which made her feel glamorous and special. She was pretty pleased with the way she looked.

Danny and Damien were coming straight from training. In a strained conversation earlier, she'd arranged to meet Damien at a nearby posh hotel for a quick pre-show drink. Claudette and Danny were also meeting there, and Claudette's plan was that all four of them could arrive together as representatives of Royal Boroughs FC.

As the car glided through the streets of London Amy could barely wait. She was excited about the premiere, but mostly she was dying to see her boyfriend again. He'd take one look at her and realize he didn't need any *space* after all.

Amy finally walked into the dim lighting of the fancy hotel lobby and instantly recognized Claudette, looking unbelievably striking in a long golden ball gown that contrasted amazingly with her dark skin. Next to her was Danny, classically handsome in one of his own-line Armani suits. But there was no sign of Damien.

'Hi,' she puffed, relieved that she hadn't encountered any paps. She was sure she was red in the face from all the hurrying. 'Where's Damien?'

Claudette looked her up and down. 'You look nice, darling. Who chose that for you?'

Amy tried to disguise her irritation. 'I did.' She turned slightly towards Danny and asked again, 'Where's Damien?'

Danny looked at Claudette.

Amy didn't like the way this was going. 'Is he OK? Wasn't he at training today?'

'Yeah, course,' Danny answered. 'But there was a – he had to go somewhere –'

'Danny, darling, just tell her. She might be a baby, but you can't sugar-coat everything for her.'

Amy's heart reached the tips of her patent leather heels. 'Tell me what?'

Danny shot Claudette a thunderous look. 'There was a – an incident a little while ago in the changing rooms at the ground.'

Claudette laughed and shook her earrings, which were gold and ultra-sparkly. 'You sound like a train announcer! Amy darling, there wasn't an *incident*. Damien punched Scott White's lights out on the pitch. He's my hero. It's about time *someone* did that.'

'It was in the changing rooms of the training ground,' Danny corrected. 'And it was barely even a ruck. More of a shouting match with girlie shoving. Fendi bags at dawn, that sort of thing.'

Claudette's eyebrows waggled crazily. 'Danny, can't you just say "handbags", like a normal man?'

'Claudy, you're the one who pushed me to be the "new face of Armani menswear"!'

Claudette ignored him and turned to Amy. 'Anyway, Scott and Damien were naughty, and Big Carl's kept them behind in detention.'

'He's just talking to them,' Danny said. 'Like a big girl's Miu Miu blouse.' He smirked at Claudette.

'Omigod, Danny, do not *ever* let me catch you saying Miu Miu again!'

'Miu Miu! Miu Miu!' Danny sounded like a deranged cat.

Claudette rolled her eyes. 'Anyway, I'm sure Scott deserved it. I wish Damien had punched him harder.'

'Oh, you'll never let it go, Claudy!'

'Big Carl picked him over you to take that penalty! It wasn't right, Danny, and you know it. You complained too.'

'Yeah, for two minutes! Not two months!'

'You keep getting benched for *him*.'

'I'm doing OK, Claudy.'

'I still think he should be off the team.' Her nostrils flared with passionate anger. 'No one gets the glory that *my man* deserves.'

Danny gazed at her with a soppy look on his face. 'Claudy, I love you, babe.'

'I love you too, darling.'

Amy squirmed while they kissed, though she wished Damien was here to do the same thing to her.

Claudette broke away from Danny and fluffed up her hair extensions with one hand. 'Amy darling, we were hoping Damien would turn up any minute, but it doesn't look like it, does it? So we'll go without him – never mind, I'm adaptable – but if anyone asks, say you can't comment. I can't stand Scott but I have nothing against Damien, and he doesn't deserve the negative publicity.'

'You're overreacting, Claudy.' Danny shrugged. 'No one cares.'

Amy was still stuck on the first part of all this, and now that her friends weren't fighting or smooching, she felt she could mention it. 'But it's impossible! Damien wouldn't get into trouble with Big Carl. He never gets aggressive. No way.' She ignored the niggle at the back of her mind – was it a coincidence that it was Paige's boyfriend he was supposedly fighting with?

Claudette raised her eyebrows. 'He's a man, Amy. What do you expect from him? They're basically apes.'

Danny beat his chest like a gorilla and pounced at Claudette. She swatted him away, squealing. Then she dusted down her dress and put her nose in the air.

'Come on, we've got red carpet to tread.'

The whole experience of going to a premiere was fantastic. Amy was dazzled as they emerged from the car and headed towards the cinema entrance amid excitedly screaming crowds and snapping photographers. They were mostly held at a safe distance by a red rope, metal barriers and a team of officials in fluorescent yellow jackets. Amy knew the people weren't cheering for her – most of them seemed to be in a frenzy and screamed even if one of the yellow-jacketed people walked near them. But it felt amazing all the same.

Claudette posed with Danny for the cameras and Amy tried to shrink into the background rather than look like a third wheel.

The film was good, too, although she was constantly distracted by the thought that Damien might walk in any minute. She missed huge chunks of the action by staring at the nearest fire exit every time it opened. She kept spotting minor celebrities as they popped out with mobile phones in their hands, and she even spotted the main actress from the film, who looked smaller and more twig-like in real life.

It wasn't Saturday night at the Stanleydale multiplex, that was for sure.

Amy tried to hide her disappointment when there was still no sign of Damien by the end of the film. Along with everybody else, she switched on her mobile the second she reached the cinema foyer, but he hadn't left her a message either. She decided to confront him at the house rather than call him – this wasn't a conversation she wanted to have over the phone.

She stifled her anger all the way through the after-party, making her excuses to leave as soon as possible. Claudette and Danny offered to drop her back at Caseydene but bickered non-stop in the back of the limo. By the time Amy got home her head was bursting with unsettled thoughts.

She couldn't see any lights glowing from the cottage but she knocked at the door all the same.

There was no answer.

Amy checked her phone – it was past midnight. No way was Damien was still being talked to by Big Carl, not if what Barbie had told her about her husband's sleeping habits was true.

She trudged back to the house, calling his number and restricting herself to three angry messages on his voicemail.

Then she told herself not to think about it any more. Damien had stood her up. Either there was a very good explanation or she had to have serious words with him, because this just wasn't on. But although she knew that, she couldn't help standing by the window with her phone in her hand, waiting for a sighting of Damien, or for some lights to go on, or for a message to bleep through on her phone.

It was nearly two in the morning when she forced herself to go to bed, still churning with a combination of fury and misery, but telling herself everything would be OK.

She woke up during a particularly vivid dream in which everything with Damien was fine. He turned up for the premiere after all, he held her hand all the way through, he whispered to her that all that 'needing space' business was rubbish and they should forget it and live together on a remote tropical island, breeding pugs to sell to Kylie Kemp and her friends. Best of all, Damien kissed her theatrically in front of the paparazzi after the film, while fireworks went off in the background. But one of the loud rockets going off woke her up, and she realized it was actually someone hammering on the wall behind her head.

She got up, slipped on a robe and padded in bare feet

towards her bedroom door. She opened it a crack and peered out. The hallway was full of men in low-slung builders' jeans, hefting barrels of paint and equipment into the room next to Amy's. She tried to retreat quickly and shut the door, but the unmistakeable blare of Barbie stopped her.

'Babe! Are you only just up? You're turning into one of us! Or worse than us! Me and Rosay were up proper early today! And she got in much later than you last night. Again! Between you and me,' Barbie lowered her voice, 'I think she's seeing someone. But if I ask her about it, she gets all shy. She disappeared the last two afternoons, too, all fired up.'

Amy tried to smile. She didn't really want to stand in her dressing gown talking about Rosay's mysterious love life to Rosay's mother.

'Anyway, sorry about the noise. I changed my mind about that room – too much cerise.' She looked thoughtful. 'You don't mind, do you, babe? Only I'm having some fixtures and fittings moved too. I thought you'd be up by now.'

'No, it's fine, honestly . . .' She nearly said 'Barbie' but suddenly the name 'Barbara-Ann' popped into her head and she had to stifle a giggle. Then she thought about how much it would tickle Damien to hear Barbie's real name, and the fact that Rosay had been called Rose. But she hadn't even spoken to him since she'd found out. The smile slid off her face.

'Thanks for sorting those party invitations. Rosay's been doing her bit this morning, working on the band thing. Maybe you two can work together later.'

'Maybe,' Amy muttered, as Barbie waved and went back to barking orders.

Amy shut the door on the chaos and headed to her en suite, feeling grateful that she didn't have to face a corridorful of builders to reach a bathroom. She checked her phone on the way, and did a double take at how late it was. This time yesterday she'd already been at the swimming pool for an hour. Whereas today . . . she only had a couple of hours before she was supposed to be meeting Josh.

She stopped at the window and gazed at the cottage, wondering whether Damien had come home at all, and why he hadn't phoned her. Of course, it was too late and he'd be at training now for the day, and probably too annoyingly well-behaved to check his phone. She wished that the firework hammer had woken her earlier and given her time to get to the cottage before Damien left for the day. She could have yelled at him.

Or at least she could have seen him.

She drew the pink and purple flowery curtain across to blot out the sight of the cottage. Then she started getting ready for lunch with Josh. He quite possibly knew something about what was going on with Damien, but no doubt wouldn't tell her.

Well, maybe she'd find a way to *make* him tell her.

19

After agreeing to pose for some quick snaps, Amy ducked down her usual alleyway to shake off Caseydene's resident paparazzi and hurried up the high street, following the directions Josh had given her yesterday. She'd dressed simply in a pair of Seven for All Mankind jeans that had turned up in a 'complimentary' parcel from a boutique store, along with a chiffon blouse she'd got from Primark last summer. A simple pair of Oasis sandals and some Missoni shades that Rosay had lent her when she arrived completed the low-key look. It was only lunch after all, and she didn't want Josh to think she'd made too much effort.

The charity shops and mobile phone outlets gradually gave way to pretty boutiques and cafes. She passed newspaper billboards and people standing at bus stops reading tabloids, and wondered momentarily if there were any photos from last night in them.

She turned into a cobbled road and was nearly at the restaurant when she had to stop right outside a newsagent to wait for some lights to change, and she gave in to her curiosity.

Stepping inside the tiny paper shop, Amy gazed straight at a line of red-topped newsprint. She spotted a pic of the glamorous and tiny actress from yesterday's premiere and smiled, picking up the paper to see if she or Claudette were in the background. Asha and Susi would go crazy with excitement if her red-carpet moment had made it into the papers.

But she didn't bother to look closer because the main headline drew her attention. '*White Love Rat: Boroughs Striker Cheats Again!*' And there was a photo of Scott White holding a hand in front of his face, outside a nightclub of some kind.

There was a tiny amount of text that mentioned rumours about Scott cheating on Paige Young. She put the paper down and picked up the one next to it, which read: '*Daily World Exclusive: SCOTT In The Act!*' The picture was damning – Scott in a passionate clinch with a tall, dark-haired girl. You couldn't see her face, but you could tell she wasn't the blonde, freckly, petite Paige Young.

The article was roughly the same as the other one, but with a lot more details. It said that Scott White had a secret girlfriend; a mystery woman who called herself Miss X. She'd sold her story – complete with text messages and recordings of her conversations with Scott – exclusively to the *Daily World*.

Amy bought the paper and left the shop, lost in her thoughts. So much for Claudette stopping photos of Boroughs players from getting into the papers if it meant negative publicity. Though this was about Scott White, so maybe it was an exception. Claudette really seemed to have a problem with him.

Amy found the restaurant and stumbled through the door, half-glued to the *Daily World*. She was reading the transcript of one of Miss X and Scott's phone calls, '*continued on page 17*'. They talked about some other team members, making some pretty harmless but funny allegations about what the players thought of each other and of their manager. All the names were replaced by rows of Xs. This only made Amy, and probably every other reader of the paper, more curious. One thing was for sure: Big Carl was going to hate this story. So was Scott White. And Paige Young.

Josh was waiting for her, already seated at a small table. The restaurant was quiet and the decor was more night-time than lunch time. The restaurant windows were darkly tinted and there were silver-grey tablecloths and lit red candles on each table. The whole atmosphere was pretty date-like. Amy forgot the Scott scandal for a second and felt butterflies leap in her stomach. What was she doing in a place like this with a boy that wasn't Damien?

Josh stood up when he saw her. He kissed her lightly on one cheek and sat back down, leaving her in a cloud of deliciously rich-smelling citrus aftershave.

'I thought you weren't coming!'

'I got distracted on the way,' Amy admitted, holding out the paper as she sat down opposite him.

Josh immediately frowned, an expression that oddly made Amy relax. This was nothing like a date. They were friends – and they both had different reasons to care about the Boroughs-related scandal that had hit the headlines. It was probably going to mean a lot of extra work for Josh, after all, if one of his main assignments was getting the team to gel, and everyone had suddenly turned against the main striker.

'Does it worry you, what you've read?' Josh asked. 'How do you feel about it?'

'You're doing it again. You're a total counsellor.' Amy smiled to show she was joking.

Josh seemed confused, and then he grinned back. He really was gorgeous.

'Sorry,' Amy added. 'I didn't mean to be rude.'

'No, *I'm* sorry. I didn't mean to be a total counsellor.'

They smiled at each other for a while.

Amy cleared her throat. 'So, uh, we'd better decide what to order, huh?'

'Yeah, OK,' Josh said, still looking straight at her.

She cast her eyes down at the menu and told herself he was being friendly and there was nothing wrong with meeting him like this. Anyway, she was here to get more information about Damien and there was no point hanging around. She couldn't think of a subtle way to introduce the subject so she just blurted, 'Damien didn't come home last night.'

'Are you sure?' Josh said, leaning closer. 'Didn't you say you'd moved out?'

Amy kept her eyes on the menu. 'Yes, but I'm just across the courtyard and I can see the cottage. Not that I look,' she added hastily. 'Usually. I'm in Barbie's guest wing, you know.'

'Oh, the one she's decorating?'

'You've heard about that?'

'She talked to me about it for an hour yesterday! That and this party she's organizing for Saturday, which is a complete nightmare and you've stepped in as a lifesaver. You and Rosay, right?'

'Yes. Separately, though.' Amy wondered how they'd moved away from the subject of Damien so quickly. At this rate, she was never going to get Josh to tell her what he knew.

'Oh, I thought you and Rosay got on?'

'We kind of did. I don't know. I heard some things . . . I'm not sure how much I trust her.'

'Yeah, you're very wise. You should get to know someone as much as possible before you trust them. First impressions aren't always enough.' He coughed. 'But sometimes they are. Sometimes you have a . . . a connection with someone, and you just know.'

Amy gulped. He couldn't possibly mean her . . . and him. Could he? She glanced up, but he was busy studying his menu and he didn't show any signs that he'd said anything out of the ordinary.

'So what are you doing for this party?' Josh asked when the waiter had taken their order. He gave her a friendly smile. 'Anything I can help with?'

'No way!' Amy shifted in her seat. 'I mean, no, it's pretty boring, and I'm sure you're busy enough. Isn't this Scott scandal going to mean extra work?'

'Yes, possibly, although it might all blow over in a day or so. I asked my dad for his professional opinion, just generally, you know. He says as long as the team stays focused and together, there isn't really an issue.'

This was Amy's chance to steer the conversation back. 'I don't know if that's going to happen. I think Danny Harris might have a problem with Scott. At least, I know his wife has. And I heard Damien had a fight with Scott yesterday.'

The waiter arrived with their drinks. Amy sipped hers as she waited for Josh to comment.

'Or did Scott have a fight with Damien?' he asked.

'Pardon?'

'You said Damien had a fight with Scott. But how do you know it wasn't the other way around? Maybe Scott was upset about something Damien had done.'

'Why? Have you heard something about it?'

Josh's silence made Amy's heart race. Could this be about Damien and Paige?

Then Josh said, 'I can't really say.'

'Right. I know. Confidentiality.' Amy sighed. Getting information about Damien out of Josh was like pulling teeth. She decided to give up trying, and with one question she got him talking about rugby and tennis instead.

Josh was expected over at the training ground in the afternoon. He said goodbye in much the same way that he'd said hello – kissing her cheek lightly and giving her a quick hug. Amy thought she heard the snap of paparazzi behind her, but when she turned she couldn't see anyone with a camera. The weirdest week of her life was clearly getting to her.

She was halfway home when she remembered that Johann's party was tonight. Would Damien still want to go after all the angry messages she'd left last night? She wondered whether the latest scandal with Paige and Scott would mean the night was cancelled anyway. If only she could speak to Damien and sort this all out. She couldn't believe they were going to have another argument when last night was meant to solve all their problems.

Amy thought she could probably check with Kylie. She didn't have Kylie's number but she remembered Paige mentioning her address: 13 Elm Street. Amy had passed Elm Street on the way here – it was a road filled with tall mansion flats that looked like they could easily be nicknamed Spooky Towers.

Well, maybe she could pop in on the way home and see if Kylie was in. They hadn't seen each other much since Amy had arrived but Kylie didn't seem like the kind of person who'd mind her coming round. There was a niggle in the back of Amy's mind – the vague idea that maybe Damien had been with Paige last night, and maybe Amy could look for signs in her flat. She tried to tell herself the whole idea was ridiculous as she headed towards the flat, but it stuck in her mind.

It took her ages to find the buzzer that read: 'Young, Kemp and P.P.'. It was only after she pressed it that she started feeling nervous. She didn't really know Kylie, and what if Paige answered and, well, said something about Damien, or . . .

The entry phone crackled. 'Stop it! Put it down! Hold on! Come in! Quick!' There was a long buzz.

Amy hesitated before pushing the heavy wooden door open. A small beige creature came hurtling towards her and licked at her ankles.

'Close it! Quick! Poshie, come here! Bad boy!'

Amy shut the door, hoping the animal, who must be Poshie Pug, hadn't escaped.

'Hi, Amy! God, I'm sorry. Bad boy!' Kylie stood with her hands on her hips. Her blonde hair was bound up in large pink curlers and she was wearing a silk robe. She bent down and scooped the small dog into her arms. 'Mummy's so cross! Quick, we'd better get in.' She hurried into the flat and Amy followed her. Once the door was safely shut, Kylie sat down on a sofa, scratching the top of Poshie's head and making soothing sounds. 'It's OK, don't cry. Mummy forgives you. But we mustn't get caught by the Spooky Gang.'

Amy couldn't quite believe what she was seeing or hearing. 'Who are the Spooky Gang?'

Kylie looked up as if she'd forgotten Amy was there. 'The people in the other flats, of course. They mostly just stare at us like zombies. But they don't know about Poshie. We're not allowed pets here.'

Poshie made a doggie rasping noise followed by a loud snort, which made Amy doubt that the neighbours, alive or living dead, hadn't noticed him.

Kylie patted him on the head. 'We smuggle you out for walkies, don't we, Poshie? All wrapped up in a blanket.'

Amy looked around. The flat was gorgeous – spacious but comfortable-looking, and also a total mess. Every cupboard was open and the contents, mostly unopened packets of food and discarded clothes, spilled out all over the floor. So much for finding clues about whether Damien had been here – it was hard to find a space to stand without treading on anything.

Kylie put Poshie down. He instantly flopped over and showed his fawn-coloured podgy tummy. 'Aw, cutie!' She tickled Poshie's fur. 'So nice to see you! Sit down!'

It took Amy a while to realize that the last two sentences were addressed to her. She picked her way through the mess to an armchair and looked at Kylie's hair. 'Uh, nice to see you, too. Sorry if I disturbed you, er, doing your hair.'

Kylie laughed and patted a curler. 'Don't be silly. I left the hairdresser's like this a few hours ago. I don't care who sees me in my rollers – I love being papped in them! It's a style thing. You should try it. I'll give you the name of my hairdresser.'

'Oh. Rico from the Delilah Salon does my hair.' Amy did a double take. Had those words actually just come out of her mouth? What would the twins say if they heard her?

'Rico at Delilah? Isn't that Claudette's hairdresser?' Kylie's already wide eyes grew even larger in amazement.

'Er, yes, she made me the appointment.'

'Omigod, well, be careful. Claudette and Paige had a massive row last year after Paige went to see Patrice at Obu once too often!'

Amy looked at her blankly.

'You know? Obu. You need an introduction to get an appointment there. Patrice was Claudette's hairdresser before Rico. But she said all these nice things about Paige in front of Claudette, and it was war! Claudette's like that witch out of Snow White, only not witchy or anything.' Kylie frowned like she was concentrating hard. 'I mean, all the people who work for her have to say she's the prettiest and best person or they're fired!' She laughed. 'Anyway, you didn't hear that from me. I don't spread rumours.'

'Oh, right.' Amy doubted that would happen with her and Rico, but it was nice to get a warning.

There was a bit of a silence then. Amy glanced nervously around the room, not quite sure what to say next. The television was on in the background, showing old music videos. Kylie followed Amy's gaze.

'Oh, I get it! You've come to ask about my aunt's reality TV thing! Did you hear that I was desperate to drop out? That would have been brilliant – thanks, Amy – Auntie Fran wouldn't let up about me doing it, but then she finally got a replacement for me, just before the rehearsal on Monday. Phew, what a relief, I love that person forever, whoever she is! I can't sing at all! Auntie Fran kept saying I shouldn't worry because neither can the others, the ones who have been rehearsing for months while I was refusing to do it, but that's not true. Well, I don't know who they all are, of course, but I know Paige is fantastic. Can you sing?'

Amy felt overwhelmed. She hadn't understood much of what Kylie had said. 'Not really.'

'Yeah, neither can I.' She gazed at Amy with her huge blue eyes. 'Wait, do you know what I'm talking about? About my aunt who's something important in television, and she's got five footballers' girlfriends or ex-girlfriends for this new programme? And the final line-up is all top secret and I'm not allowed to mention it to anyone?'

Amy stared at her. 'Er, no.'

Kylie gave a serious nod. 'Well, I'd better not tell you anything about it, then. Paige and Courtney, the goalie's girl-friend, are in it, plus some others that even I don't know about. Auntie Fran said the publicity machine is well in motion already, whatever that means.' She crossed her eyes in a puzzled expression that didn't stop her face from looking flawless. 'Anyway, I didn't tell you anything. I'm good at keeping secrets.'

'Oh,' said Amy. 'OK.'

'So why *are* you here?' Kylie asked, tickling Poshie.

'Er, I just came to ask about tonight. Whether it's still on, I mean, what with everything that's happened.'

'Oh, yes, poor Paige.'

Amy nodded as sympathetically as she could manage.

'But at least she's used to it,' Kylie added. 'She's dealt with it for quite a while now and she's coping pretty well.'

'Wow, really?' So it was true that Scott had cheated on Paige? It sounded like it had been happening for ages, and Paige knew all about it.

'She keeps insisting she's OK about it,' Kylie said. 'She's been keeping it all secret for months, but I suppose it was going to get out eventually, especially the way things have been going lately.'

Amy nodded again.

Kylie stroked Poshie's fur. 'At least she has Damien now. It's made it all a lot easier for her, especially lately.'

Amy sat up. 'What?' Her heart started beating very fast. 'How do you mean?'

Kylie continued calmly. 'Well, I know Damien was with her last night, for example. He stayed over.' Then she hesitated, narrowing her huge blue eyes at Amy. She looked like a china doll, slowly blinking. 'Wait. You *do* know about this, don't you?'

Amy reminded herself to keep breathing. She had to be missing something. How could Kylie be sitting there and calmly telling her that Damien was seeing Paige? 'You mean about . . .?'

'About Paige and Damien. And last night.' She nudged her head to one side meaningfully. 'You know?'

Amy stood up shakily. She *must* be misunderstanding this. 'Damien was here last night?' she said, just to check.

Kylie rolled her eyes. 'Yeah, he slept here. With Paige. I thought I said that. And they say *I'm* stupid. No offence,

Amy. What's the matter?' Then she groaned and put her head in her hands. 'Omigod, you didn't know, did you?'

'Sorry, I've just remembered I – I have to go.'

Amy stumbled towards the door. Poshie made it there before her and snuffled around her feet.

'Hang on a minute! Don't let Poshie out.'

Amy hesitated with her hand on the door handle.

Kylie appeared by the door. 'You spoilt dog! You always get your own way. Mummy will take you for walkies to Daddy Johann's soon, promise.' She picked the dog up and turned to Amy. 'You know, you're still welcome at Johann's tonight as long as you don't say anything about, well, you know. What I just told you by mistake. The last thing, I mean. Believe it or not, I haven't mentioned it to Johann. Paige asked me not to and I'm a good friend. I don't spill people's secrets.' Kylie batted her long lashes. 'Anyway, I'm sure Damien would have told you sooner or later. Just don't tell anyone else, will you, if that's OK with you?'

Amy couldn't believe what Kylie was asking her to do. Was this what it was to be a footballer's girlfriend? Turning a blind eye to your boyfriend cheating on you, pretending everything was OK? Paige had been ignoring Scott's affair, and now Amy was supposed to ignore Damien's?

'You are coming round, aren't you? Paige and Damien are definitely coming, and it would be great if you could make it too.' Kylie turned her big eyes on Amy. Poshie did the same, his wrinkly pug-face equally imploring.

Amy gulped a big breath. *Paige and Damien?* She was supposed to think of them as a couple already? She felt sick. But Kylie was being so casual about it all, like it was nothing!

'Uh, thanks, but I don't think I'm free tonight. I've . . . really got to go, sorry.'

She shut the door quickly even though Poshie was in Kylie's arms and in no danger of escaping. Then she leant against the wall and burst into tears.

20

As Amy jumped into a passing cab and made her way back to Caseydene, the ache of shock and misery was slowly replaced by anger.

Damien was cheating on her! He'd stayed with Paige last night! He'd lied to her, going on about 'space' and all kinds of nonsense, and making her feel she was wrong to accuse him of having feelings for Paige, when she'd clearly been right all along!

Well, one thing was for sure. It was all over between her and Damien. Amy wasn't like Paige – she wasn't going to put up with it.

She couldn't believe this was happening to her. It felt like the end of the world.

She checked the time on her phone. Asha would be on lifeguard duty and her phone would be safely in her locker, but Susi might have her phone set to vibrate in her pocket, in the cafe. She did that sometimes, and she'd sneakily check it and pop outside for a quick phone break if things were quiet.

Amy sent her a text that made it clear this was an emergency. It said, 'Damien cheating. Official.' She needed her friends more than ever right now.

The cab approached the main gates of Caseydene when her phone rang and she heard Asha and Susi talking together, obviously both crowded around the same phone.

'Come home, love! Just get on a train right now, this second, don't look back!'

Amy felt the tears well up again at the sounds of their voices. 'I should . . . I should speak to him first, shouldn't I? Hear his side, right?' She sniffed. But what could his side possibly be? He'd spent the night with Paige – Kylie had said so!

Asha said, 'No! Forget him right now! Just come home.'

At the same time, Susi said, 'Yeah, make him explain. Make him suffer!'

Then Asha and Susi started arguing with each other about the right thing to do.

Amy sniffed, wanting to smile at her bickering friends but not quite managing it.

'Hey, you two. I'll call you,' she promised. 'As soon as I know what I'm doing.'

'Amy, take care. We love you – uh-oh.'

'What's happening?'

She heard Asha whisper, 'Big Ears! Got to go! Call us later!'

The phone went dead.

As the gates slid open to let the car into the grounds Amy checked the time again. When would Damien be back? She wasn't even sure. Maybe he'd never be back. Maybe he'd moved in with Paige.

She let herself into the house, barely nodded at Eva and rushed up to her room.

She grabbed her swimming things and ran to the pool, relieved to find she had the sports complex to herself. She really didn't feel like being counselled by Josh right now.

She swam for ages, pounding the water hard as she cut angrily through length after length. Eventually she hauled herself out of the water, surprised to find she still didn't feel any better.

Back in the pink and purple room, she dragged her monster suitcase out of the cupboard she'd wedged it into only two days ago. She was about to turn out the wardrobe when her phone rang.

The display said 'Damien'.

She stared at it for a few seconds. She didn't feel ready for this. But would she ever be?

She took a deep breath and answered. 'Damien.'

'Ames! At last! God, I'm so sorry about last night! This is the first chance I've had to call you!'

Amy sat on the bed. She'd almost forgotten that he'd stood her up at the premiere last night, her head was so full of the other, much worse stuff. But he sounded so normal, so Damien-ish. She clutched the phone to her ear, wishing he would tell her Kylie had got it all wrong, wishing everything could be all right again between them.

'I got your messages and I know you must be really angry with me. I'm so sorry – I can explain, I promise.'

'Where were you?' she asked dully, but with a note of hope in her voice.

'Oh, God, Ames, I don't know where to begin! We got kept behind after training –'

'All of you? Or just you and Scott?'

There was a silence. Then Damien said, 'Did Danny tell you about that? Look, just listen to me. Something happened and —'

'And were you kept behind *all night*?'

Another silence. Then Damien's voice, colder. 'No, not all night. But I was . . . delayed. A lot.'

Oh, yeah, thought Amy. 'With Paige, right?' she said as calmly as she could. She felt that rage again, coursing through her blood, throbbing in her head.

But before she could say anything else, Damien had the nerve to sound indignant. 'Amy, you're doing it *again*. You sound like you're accusing me. You don't even know you're doing it, do you?'

She wanted to scream and throw her phone across the room. Instead she took a deep breath and said, 'Damien, I'll give you one chance to tell me the truth about what you were really doing last night, and who you were doing it with. *All night*. And all of the truth.'

The silence was even longer this time and Amy thought her head might explode. Or possibly her heart.

Damien's voice was small. 'Amy, it's complicated.'

'Why? It seems pretty easy to me. Just tell me you were with Paige, if that's where you were.' She took a deep breath. 'So where were you?'

'I was . . . I was with Paige.'

Amy screwed her eyes shut.

'Listen, Amy! I can't . . .'

'Can't *what*, Damien? Can't admit you're cheating on me? Can't believe I'm stupid enough to have come all this way to spend time with you when you *want space*, you stand me up and then you stay out all night with some other girl?' Her voice cracked then – she couldn't help it. 'Damien Taylor, I never ever want to see you again! Don't call, don't come round, don't, don't . . . I mean it!' She hung up quickly before he heard her cry. She didn't want to give him the satisfaction. She switched her phone off so he couldn't call her back.

Or possibly so that she wouldn't wait pathetically for it to ring, staring at the picture of her and Damien in love, smiling up from the display.

Then she threw herself on the bed and took her anger out on the pillow.

21

Amy wasn't sure how much time had passed when she heard a soft knock at the door.

Rosay's voice said gently, 'Amy? Can I come in?'

'No! Go away!' Amy called, slightly surprised at her own rudeness, but also past caring.

'Fine. Suit yourself,' Rosay said more harshly, and Amy heard heels clicking down the corridor.

Good, she thought. She bashed her pillow again.

Ten seconds later, the heels were back. 'Listen. Mum says if you don't let me in, she's coming to speak to you herself and she won't take no for an answer.'

Amy sat up and wiped her eyes on the sleeve of her top. She caught a glimpse of herself in the full-length mirror on the back of the door. She looked a tear-stained mess, but that wasn't as bad as how she felt.

There was no way she could cope with Barbie in this state. There was no way she could cope with Rosay either, but she seemed the lesser of the two evils.

'Amy?'

'OK, come in.' She found a box of pink tissues, took one and started dabbing at her face.

She expected Rosay to bound in and sit on the bed like last time, but instead she hung around by the door.

'Hi. Are you OK? Well, obviously not. Mum heard you over the sound of her own voice.' Rosay gave a nervous laugh. 'Is there anything I can do? What happened?'

'It's exactly what you said would happen,' Amy said, wondering why she sounded so flat and bitter – like she blamed Rosay. She knew this wasn't Rosay's fault.

She made herself say it out loud, like picking a scab. 'Damien cheated on me with Paige.'

'Are you sure? Sure it's not another rumour?'

Amy nodded and waited for Rosay to say, 'I told you so'.

'Oh, Amy, I'm so sorry. I can't believe he'd do that!' Rosay wrinkled her nose. 'I *can* believe her, but I still hoped she wouldn't. God, and to think I've almost felt sorry for her for the last couple of days, knowing the Scott stuff was going to hit the headlines.'

'You knew about that before?'

Rosay's eyes darted around. 'No.'

'You said you knew the Scott stuff was going to hit the headlines.'

'Oh.' Rosay coughed. 'Sorry, I meant today, when it *did* hit the headlines. I saw it . . . today. In the paper. At the same time that everyone else saw it.'

'No, you knew before, didn't you?' Amy felt bold all of a sudden. It was as if finding out Damien was cheating meant she didn't care any more about being polite. After all, she'd be leaving Caseydene now. It didn't matter what Rosay thought of her; soon she'd have nothing more to do with this mad world. 'Claudette told me, remember? I know about your dad, and how he pays you to tip off the paparazzi. I suppose you know all the stories before they break, don't you?'

Rosay babbled nervously. 'No. I wish it was that easy. Dad does pictures, not words. Depending on the story, I sometimes have an idea, but he doesn't always tell me, anyway. He treats me like I'm about three.'

Amy refused to feel sorry for her. 'Except that he employs you to spy on your friends.'

Rosay shook her head. 'I don't spy! I help them out – they *want* the publicity! And he only gives me money to annoy Mum and Carlo. You can't believe Claudette. She only wants to know you if there's something in it for her.' She twiddled the door handle. 'Anyway, I'm not doing anything like that now. I stopped, thanks to you. Seriously, Amy, I've felt really bad about it since you got here and were instantly so ... trusting and friendly. It didn't seem right any more. Besides you ... kind of talked me into something else, even though you didn't know it. And that's taking up all my time now, and paying me too. I'm much happier.'

'Huh,' said Amy. *Whatever*, she thought. She didn't feel 'trusting and friendly' right now, that was for sure.

'Look, Amy, I'm really sorry about Paige and Damien. I had no idea and I know *exactly* how you feel, and if there's anything I can do –'

'What, you mean, like get *revenge*? I don't go around slashing people's clothes like a spoilt brat when I don't get my way!'

As soon as Amy said it, she wished she hadn't. What was the matter with her? It was one thing to stop worrying about politeness and quite another to go blatantly attacking Rosay, even if she was moving out.

Also, if she was honest, the idea of ripping up Paige's clothes was vaguely appealing right now. And destroying everything Damien ever cared about, and generally trampling over anyone who got in her way. Really, she could sympathize with Rosay more than ever.

Rosay looked like she'd been slapped.

Then, to Amy's surprise, instead of storming off or shouting at her or doing something Amy probably deserved after that comment, Rosay set her face in a determined grimace.

She came over and sat on Amy's bed. 'OK, Amy. I know you're upset. And, listen, I don't mind if you take it out on me. I've been through this, and it turned me into a bitch, too.' She gave Amy a small smile. 'No offence. So go on, give me what you've got! It's good for you, and I can take it. Believe me. I've had worse. All those girls have been on at me for over a year now for something I didn't even do.'

Amy nearly said, 'Yeah, right!' but she stopped herself. She felt thrown. Was it possible that Rosay was innocent? She wasn't sure. This whole tiresome mess was like a minefield of accusations.

'You don't believe me, do you? You think I did that thing to Paige, don't you?'

Amy decided to be totally honest. 'It's just that . . . I don't trust you,' she said.

'I don't blame you.' Rosay shrugged. 'OK, that's a start. Go on. You're supposed to be having a go at me! That wasn't nearly enough to make you feel better. *Why* don't you trust me? List the reasons, the bitchier the better.'

Amy found herself smiling slightly, in spite of everything. 'You owe me money.'

'I know. You're right. I shouldn't have let you buy me those clothes.'

'You *tricked* me into buying them!'

Rosay looked horrified. 'Oh no! I can't believe you saw it like that! I thought we were friends! Friends help each other out! It was a loan!' She stopped herself. 'Wait.' She comically readjusted her face into a saintly smile. 'Sorry, you're *supposed* to be getting angry with me. Pretend I didn't say that. But, listen, I said I'd pay you back, and I will. I have the money now – I really do.' She pulled out a crumpled piece of paper and showed it to Amy.

'What's that?' asked Amy.

'Bank statement. The money's gone in – I checked. And look how much there is! I'll pay you. I swear on my Gucci handbag, and honestly, Amy, it's my favourite.'

Amy shrugged. Money didn't seem that important now anyway.

'I'm still taking it on the chin.' Rosay stuck her chin out. 'Go on. Keep it coming. What else?'

'You stole my Chloé dress and chopped it up.' Amy wondered why that didn't feel so important any more either.

'I looked for a replacement!'

'So you *admit* that you chopped it up!'

'It was an experiment! I thought I'd try a bit of dressmaking to help with my limited funds thing. Besides, you couldn't have worn it as a dress, not after I wore it to the party and everyone saw it. But as a skirt . . . Except that it turns out I'm not very good, and it was a terrible skirt. Anyway, I asked the assistant at Orange County for a new dress like it, after I sent you out of the changing rooms – I thought if I found one, I could hide it with the other clothes and distract you when they rang it up. But they didn't have it.' Rosay hung her head. 'I've hunted for it in loads of places since then.'

'But I loved that dress! I want it back in one piece! I want it now!' Amy said, not caring that she sounded like the spoilt brat she'd just accused Rosay of being.

Rosay smiled. 'It's on its way now! I found one on eBay and, er, used Dad's PayPal account to buy it.'

Amy looked at her.

'Well, I had to! I haven't got a credit card. But I can pay him back now, too. Anyway, it's taken me all week on the computer, placing bids and stuff, while I've been pretending to do that party thing for Mum.'

'OK,' Amy sighed. 'Well, that's another thing. You're a liar!'

'I don't think lying to Mum counts,' Rosay mumbled. 'Everyone lies to their parents.'

'It does! I don't! And anyway, you lied to *me* about the dress!'

'You get used to lying a lot, when you're me.' Rosay shrugged one shoulder miserably. 'No one ever believes a word I say anyway, so I figure I might as well.'

'Well . . . you shouldn't.' Amy sniffed.

'I don't even know I'm doing it. It's usually pretty harmless, I swear. They're white lies.'

'But they're not! If you lied to your mum about helping with the party, it means there's more for me to do.'

'I've almost done what I said I'd do! The band is nearly sorted.' Rosay hit Amy lightly on the arm. 'Hey, does that mean you'll stay to help with the party? You should stay. It would make things awkward for Paige and Damien, for a start!'

Amy thought about it. Her instinct was to run away from the horror of Damien being with Paige, but why should she take off like a guilty person? She'd done nothing wrong. And she'd put all that hard work into the party. She should at least go to it! But she didn't know how she'd feel about seeing Damien there. Would he go with Paige? That would be too much.

Also, she needed her friends and family right now. Rosay was being really nice in her own warped way – Amy could see that. But it wasn't the same as being with Asha and Susi, who she trusted completely and could say anything to. Tears sprang to her eyes again.

Rosay smiled sadly at her. 'Amy, I know you don't owe me a thing and you think I'm a con-artist and a criminal and you hate me. But *please* stay! At least for the party.'

'I don't hate you,' Amy said, and she realized it was true. 'But I don't know about staying. When everyone hears about me and Damien it will just be embarrassing to be there. I mean, why would I still be invited?'

'Oh, please, please!' Rosay bounced on the bed. 'It won't be like that at all. Come as my guest! I promise I'll try not to lie to you any more. Or anyone. It's going to be hard. Habit of a lifetime.' She gave Amy a wry smile. 'So what do you think? Will you stay?'

'I miss home,' Amy said.

'But a few more days won't matter. Anyway, I'll miss *you*. You've been a great friend. Honestly – you've given me the confidence to do things I've always wanted to do.'

There was a commotion downstairs – someone was knocking at the door and shouting a lot.

Rosay ignored the noise. 'Also, Claudette said you didn't badmouth me when she told you everything. And you could have – you had every reason to. I probably would have, in your Christian Louboutins.' She smirked. 'As Danny Harris would say.'

Amy laughed faintly in spite of herself. 'You know, though, I don't get it. Are you friends with Claudette or not? Am I supposed to trust her with stuff, or not? I can't work out who's telling the truth around here.'

Rosay gave a wise nod. 'Ah, see *that's* the game. You're learning to play it.'

Amy looked at her.

'Anyway, I can tell you the rules. I learned them the hard way. There's only one person you can trust.' She paused dramatically and said in an American-sounding drawl, 'Yourself.' Then she laughed. 'OK, and me. At least, sometimes.'

Amy smiled. Rosay was crazy and a pain, but she was oddly likeable. At least, sometimes.

'As for Claudette,' Rosay continued. 'She's the best game-player of the lot. She's only ever out for herself, and never lets any friendship worries stand in the way of getting exactly what she wants. She truly doesn't care!'

The noise grew louder and Rosay wandered over to the window. She peered out. 'I warned you that first Saturday that you have to be careful what you tell her. She has a hotline to a brilliant PR guy who refuses to listen to anyone but her. Between you and me, I think he's besotted with her. It's like she has total control of which stories get out and which don't.

She's the reason I lost everything last year.' She sighed. 'The only thing this guy loves more than Claudette is money – but it takes a lot of it. Luckily, someone came along this week with enough to get past her. And it sorted me out in the bargain.'

'What do you mean?' asked Amy.

'OK, this is top, top, top secret, right? But I'm dying to tell someone. And maybe if I trust you, it will help you to trust me, or something.'

'Er, yeah,' Amy muttered. 'Maybe.'

'OK, it's like this.' Rosay lowered her voice. 'It's to do with Miss X.'

Amy gasped. 'Are *you* Miss X?'

Rosay smiled mysteriously. 'In a way. I can explain. Promise you won't say anything?'

Amy didn't even manage to promise before she got an even bigger shock. Her bedroom door burst open and some familiar faces appeared – no, crash-landed – in her room amid screams of, 'Amy! You poor lamb! Where is he? I'll kill him!'

Amy was delighted to hear the Stanleydale accent, standing out a mile here at Caseydene.

She threw her arms around each of her best friends in turn. 'Susi! Asha! What are you doing here?'

'Big Ears sacked us!' Asha moaned.

'Yeah, for talking to *you*!' Susi added, nudging Amy.

'Oh God, no! I'm sorry!'

'Don't be sorry! I'm made up! It's worth it,' said Asha.

'You're more important,' added Susi.

'So I said to Susi, blow this! Let's get the next train to London.'

'And I said to Asha, you're crazy.'

'And Mum said, the pair of you are getting on my nerves. Go and stay with Uncle Dinesh for a few days and you can check on Amy. I'll pay your train fare if you look after him.'

'We have to wash his socks!' moaned Asha.

'We do not! We have to do his shopping and a bit of cooking, and try to persuade him to come and live with Mum. And we have to get back to Uncle Dinesh's soon, Ash.'

'We have to talk to Amy first. Amy! Amy! I can't believe this place! Your dad gave me the address when I told him we were surprising you.' Asha gave her friend another hug. 'By the way, he says hello and ring your mum. Wow, it's so amazing here! Where's that annoying girl you were talking about?'

Amy blushed. 'Asha!' she said. 'I, er –'

But Rosay laughed. 'Cheers, Amy. So you're the famous twins?' she asked. 'I've heard so much about you. Where did you get that top? It's heavenly!'

'This?' Susi beamed, pulling at the red and gold embroidery. 'You're crazy! It's Asda! You know, the one Coleen Rooney promotes? You don't know her, do you?'

Asha hit her playfully on the arm. 'Susi, I can't believe you asked that. You're so uncool sometimes.'

'Sounds like a Japanese designer,' said Rosay, smiling. 'Is it couture?'

'Amy, tell me she's joking.' Asha poked her. 'She's joking, isn't she?'

Amy nodded and smiled. She realized she hadn't felt this happy in ages. With friends like these, she could almost forget that the love of her life had left her for another girl.

22

'You didn't tell me this place was crawling with fit men!' Asha said, pressing her nose against the window of Barbie's study. 'I would have got myself sacked sooner! Never mind the male Water World lifeguards – *who* is he?'

Asha and Amy were on party duty. Susi was with Uncle Dinesh and Rosay was . . . well, wherever Rosay went to shirk. She was probably off with Scott White, or something, if it was true that she was Miss X. Amy had tried to confirm that with her, but Rosay said she'd changed her mind about telling Amy. She just kept saying it would all be clear soon enough. And she carried on disappearing at regular intervals.

'Amy, I'm talking to you!'

Amy looked up from the seating plan she was buried in and followed Asha's gaze, even though she had a pretty good idea of who it would be. After all, there were only two fit lads who hung around Caseydene, and it couldn't be Damien. She hadn't seen or heard from him at all since the argument. And she hadn't been staring out of the window at the cottage, either. Well, not *all* the time.

'Amy. Fittie! Tell me who he is! Now!'

Amy sighed. 'It's the team psychologist.'

'Oi, fit lad! Over here! Come and analyse me!' Asha made kissy noises at the window.

'Asha! What are you *like*?'

Asha laughed. 'So what's his name and when can I snog him?'

'Asha!'

'OK, OK, *meet* him. He *is* invited, isn't he?' She picked up the place cards that Susi had carefully written out yesterday in her precise, curling handwriting. 'Is he called Danny Harris?' Asha was hopeless. She knew nothing about football. 'Is he Johann Haag? Is he Damien . . . oh.'

Amy took the cards out of Asha's hands and tried not to think about where they'd seat Damien. Somewhere miles away from Paige, that was for sure. Or would that look too obvious? Maybe she should seat them together and show the world that she was bigger than that. But how was she going to stand to watch that, right in front of her? The thought was unbearable!

'I've decided,' said Amy, thinking fast. 'It's going to be a stand-up buffet.' She tore up the seating plan. 'I'll talk to the caterers.'

'Good idea, though Susi might be a bit miffed about the cards. But she can take it.' Asha smirked. The she picked up a card. 'Paige Young,' she read. 'Surely *she's* not coming?'

'The invitations went out before I found out.'

Asha gave her a hug and said mean things about Paige that made Amy smile, even though they probably weren't true, and anyway, it was Damien she was really angry with. It had been seriously brilliant having her friends here for the last few days. They'd let her rant and they'd made angry threats in all the right places and generally made her feel better.

Barbie had been beyond kind, too. She said Amy could stay as long as she liked and she even offered Asha and Susi a room each, after which Susi had dragged Asha, practically screaming, back to tend to Uncle Dinesh's socks.

Even Rosay had been great. She hadn't been around much, but she'd stayed true to her word and given Amy the clothes money she'd promised. She'd also brought her the paper every morning to prove that the world wasn't being told about Paige and Damien. Instead, the papers were full of the Miss X and Scott White story, which was now mostly breaking online and then being picked up and spread through the tabloids. *Goss-Monger.com* was posting a daily blog called 'Texts From Miss X' – messages that were packed with juicy gossip about other footballers. Yesterday's post had named and shamed a couple of members of a rival team for cheating on their girlfriends. One thing was for sure – whoever Miss X was, Rosay or not, she seemed to be a crusader for footballers' girlfriends, determined to reveal the truth about behaviour she thought the players had 'got away with'.

The papers also featured confessions from Scott White's '*other* other women', who seemed to be in large supply. Then there was the story of Paige Young dumping Scott White. She was quoted as saying, 'He broke my heart.' This was followed by comments from the public, which ranged from 'she had it coming, Mum says she's a total lush' (Jaz, aged 15) to 'he obviously drove her to drink, poor love' (Betty, aged 68).

Amy supposed she should feel sorry for her. But the truth

was, she felt sick at the thought that Paige was officially single and free to go out with her boyfriend. Her *ex*-boyfriend.

Amy missed Damien. She missed him like crazy and she couldn't believe everything had all gone so horribly wrong. She was set to go back to Stanleydale with the twins the day after the party. The three of them were planning on finding another summer job somewhere. It might be fun, but it wouldn't be the August that Amy had looked forward to for all these weeks.

Damien hadn't tried to contact her, either because she'd been so forceful on the phone that day, or because he didn't care. She nearly weakened a few times, nearly strode over to the cottage to confront him, though she was slightly worried that she'd end up begging him to take her back. Or that Paige would be there. It was just as well Asha, Susi or sometimes Rosay caught her and distracted her each time she'd been tempted.

'Aw, the fittie's gone!' Asha complained. 'Where's he gone? Come back!'

'He'll be at the tennis court. There's a pool right next to it,' Amy said. 'Why don't you check it out, Ash?'

'Brilliant idea! You're a genius! I'll *check it out* all right,' Asha smiled. 'And I'll look at the pool, too. Can I have a swim there later, if I get my stuff?'

'Yeah, I'm sure it's no problem,' Amy said, but Asha was already halfway out of the door with a huge smile on her face.

Left on her own, Amy rang the caterers to tell them about the proposed changes, and then she put the finishing touches to the rest of the party plans. She confirmed that the security was booked, and the parking arranged, and she finalized everything with the employment agency where she'd paid extra to hire last-minute waiters and waitresses.

Amy busied herself with the last thing on her list, which was the only thing she hadn't managed to do yet. She'd cancelled the party's connection with Barbie's chosen charity, the Royal Clinic for Cosmetic Surgery, without much protest from Barbie, who'd said, 'Oh, well, it's not like I don't pay them enough anyway! And there will be plenty more in it for them, the older and more young-looking I get, if you know what I mean!'

But she hadn't yet managed to invite a rep from Breast Cancer Aid, the charity she'd chosen to replace the plastic surgery clinic.

This time she was more successful – on the first try, she managed to get put through to the right department for publicity. They'd be fundraising on the night and she thought Barbie could present them with one of those huge cheques.

When she hung up, satisfied, she realized she also needed to invite the press. They needed some photos and newspaper coverage. But it had to be of the right sort – none of the guests could afford to have the place crawling with scandal-seekers.

Amy looked at her phone. She had Claudette's number, from the visits to the spa. Maybe it would be a good idea to ask Claudette. After all, Claudette had said she could arrange positive publicity and keep negative stuff out of the papers.

She dialled Claudette's number.

'Hello,' Claudette's unmistakeable voice drawled. 'I'm at the spa, make it quick!'

'Claudette, it's Amy.'

'I know it's you, baby. Caller display.'

Amy ignored the teasing tone in Claudette's voice. She explained why she was calling.

Claudette made approving noises. 'I'm surprised it's not for Breast *Implant* Aid like last year's benefit!' she laughed.

Amy didn't say that it nearly had been.

'Sure, Amy baby, I'll see what my PR guy can do. And thanks for the invites, too. Danny and I are looking forward to the party.'

'Great. OK, well . . .'

'So, about my PR guy . . .' Claudette said meaningfully.

'Yes?'

'Well. Anything else he can do for you?'

'Er, no, I don't think so. Thanks.'

'So this call wasn't an excuse to ask me about something else?'

'No.'

'You can't think of a time recently when you might have been papped doing something – well, something you shouldn't be doing?'

'No.' Amy started to feel wary. 'I have no idea what you're talking about.'

Claudette sounded surprised. 'So you don't want me to do anything about the photos?'

Amy's mind whirled. 'What photos?'

'He's a good-looking man, isn't he? And a good listener – I've bent his ear myself once or twice. But not in the same way as *you*. You're a dark horse, baby Amy!'

Amy's heart thudded. 'What are you talking about?'

'Oh, come on, you must know what I mean. Or do you do this so often that you've forgotten?' Claudette laughed.

'I've got a photo of you and Josh sharing an intimate-looking kiss outside a secluded restaurant. It's an amateur picture, but it's pretty good. A member of the public tried to get money for it. Luckily my PR guy intercepted it.'

Amy's heart sank. So she hadn't imagined it, the click of a photo being snapped the other day when she'd been with Josh? But the photo must have been taken at a misleading angle, or altered in some way, for Claudette to believe there was really something going on.

Amy thought about Asha, who was probably chatting up Josh right now. It made her feel weird. Amy wondered if she could be jealous, or just confused. She *liked* Josh, but . . .

'But nothing happened, Claudette. Honestly,' she said.

'That's not what it looks like.' Claudette gave a huge, sad sigh. 'Josh would be in big trouble, of course,' she said. 'The press will think he took advantage of you when he was supposed to be working with you and Damien. He'll never work for a sports team again. Big Carl will get slated for hiring an unqualified friend of the family in an important role. He'll probably have to resign, too.'

'Oh,' Amy mumbled. 'Right. OK. Well, what do I have to do to keep it out of the papers?' She couldn't believe she was saying this. 'Do I have to . . . pay your publicist?'

'Don't worry, darling, it's on me. For the good of the Boroughs.'

It was only when Amy let her breath out that she realized she'd been holding it. 'Oh, thanks, Claudette.'

'But listen, I'd like a little something in return. I'm curious about Rosay. She's gone all secretive on me. She's stopped tipping off the paps altogether and she won't tell me *anything*.

Has she come into some money? Is there something I should know?'

Amy wondered if her heart could sink any lower. Right now it was threatening to escape from the open toe of the brand-new sandals she'd treated herself to yesterday, when she'd taken Asha shopping for some retail therapy. Her credit card was becoming another one of her best friends.

'About Rosay?' she asked.

'Yes, darling, you've got it. What is Rosay hiding? I can't stand not knowing things. If it's to do with my team, it concerns me. I think you could shed some light on it for me. Am I right? It has something to do with Miss X, doesn't it?'

'I don't . . . I don't know,' Amy said, trying to escape what she knew was coming.

Then Claudette laughed. 'Well, be a darling and find out for me, would you? See you at the party. I'll give you until then to tell me everything.'

Amy felt sick at the slightly threatening tone in her voice.

'And Amy?'

'Yes?' she stammered.

'If you don't, the picture will look great blown up in *Just Gossip* magazine next week.'

23

It didn't matter that it poured with rain on the afternoon before the big pre-season party. Or that Miss X had revealed another set of past Boroughs indiscretions that morning on *GossMonger.com*, proving that the team was just as busy off the pitch as on it.

The important thing was that Asha, Susi and Amy, with occasional guest appearances by Rosay, had everything completely sorted for tonight. It was going to be the party to end all parties.

As the afternoon wore on, the storm died down. The fallout from the gossip didn't. Amy hadn't had time to look at the website, but she'd heard Big Carl stomping around the house. She'd also had Claudette phoning to remind her that they had a deal and she was ready to hear what exactly Rosay knew about this whole 'situation'.

Amy ignored Big Carl, and brushed off the self-appointed Head WAG's snooty tone with a casual 'I'll talk to you later, Claudette'. She hadn't found out any more about Rosay and Miss X and she wasn't sure what she was going to do about the whole Josh thing, but right now she was pushing those thoughts to the back of her mind and concentrating on preparing for the party. Maybe she didn't care about the photo anyway – Damien probably wouldn't.

The twins brought their party clothes and make-up over from Uncle Dinesh's. They dragged them, giggling, up to Amy's room, and the three of them got ready together to the blaring soundtrack of Asha's latest mix CD. It was like Saturday night in Stanleydale, only glitzier, and Amy was relishing every second of it. She even managed to stop staring out of the window at Damien's cottage for up to five whole minutes at a time.

After a while, Rosay joined them, liberally giving out make-up and clothing advice until Asha remarked, 'I've been getting myself dressed for years, love. I don't really need you to tell me how to do it. No offence.'

It could have gone either way, but Rosay burst out laughing. Then, when the twins retreated outside to take a call from their mother – 'if she hears that music she'll know we're not having a quiet night in with Uncle D' – Rosay gave Amy the green Chloé dress, which had arrived that morning from eBay.

'Thanks for understanding,' she said. 'You're a real friend – and your mates aren't bad either, although they're a bit earthier than I'm used to.'

Amy thanked her and put the dress to one side. She had to hand it to Rosay – it was an exact replica of her old favourite. But the truth was, she had many more glamorous, more up-to-date outfits to choose from now. In a sudden wave of affection, she asked Rosay to choose a dress for her to wear that night. 'As long as you let me decide on the shoes,' she added. 'And the make-up. And the jewellery, and what I drink, and who I speak to.'

Rosay looked indignant. 'I'm not that bossy!'

'Yes, you are.' Amy smiled.

Rosay rummaged through the clothes that Amy had bought with Asha. She picked up a red off-the-shoulder Jean Paul Gaultier dress that Amy knew would be perfect.

'I've got some Jimmy Choos that would go perfectly with this', she said, handing over the dress. 'So, did you see the gossip sites this morning?'

'Is this where you finally tell me the truth about Miss X?' Amy asked. Her heart pounded at the thought that she needed to report whatever Rosay said to Claudette.

'You'll find out later, I promise.'

Amy stared intently at the dress. 'I'd really love to know now.'

Rosay sighed. 'OK, I'll tell you.' She shrugged. 'I trust you not to tell anyone else. But first, listen, about today's post. Did you see what it said?'

'No.' Amy was still having trouble looking Rosay in the eye after what she'd asked.

Rosay didn't seem to notice. 'It was about Marc Frampton. My Marc.' She looked less hurt and bitter than she usually did when she said Marc's name.

'You mean it was it about Marc and . . . Paige?' Amy asked.

Rosay shook her head. 'There was a text proving that Marc was in love with someone else. Beginning with "P", like I saw. But not Paige.' She frowned. 'Pablo Something-Something. Used to play up north. A *boy*. Imagine! Marc was secretly in love with another footballer! That was why he broke up with me. Nothing to do with Paige.' She hesitated. 'Or me.'

'Oh, wow!' Amy wondered what that meant for Rosay. All

that jealousy – the damage she'd done to Paige's clothes – and she'd been wrong all along!

'I should have known. He had better taste than to go for Paige,' Rosay said. 'I bet that Pablo's proper buff.'

Amy looked at her in disbelief. Rosay was unreal!

'What? Anyway, Paige is still a boyfriend-stealer! There's still . . .' She trailed off. 'Well, she still stole Trina Santos's boyfriend, didn't she? We all know that's true. She deserved everything she got! Even though I didn't do it.'

Amy shook her head at her friend, but she couldn't help laughing a tiny bit.

'So now let me tell you about Miss X, if you're really determined to spoil the surprise for yourself,' Rosay said.

She launched into an explanation that was a million miles away from anything Amy could have guessed.

But before she could comment on it, Barbie shouted from downstairs. Though she could have been at Stadium Gardens and they'd still have heard her. 'Girls, come here! I need you here, right now! All four of you.'

Rosay groaned. 'What now?'

After rounding up the twins, Rosay and Amy found Barbie in Caseydene's main reception room, which had been totally transformed. There were clutches of white roses in small vases scattered across the room, a buffet of delicious-looking food adorned with stunning decorations, ice buckets of champagne at every turn. There was an eager team of waiting staff making final preparations, and an allocated area behind the main party room, which would soon be used by the excellent masseurs that Amy had hired from the spa for head and shoulder massages.

The adjoining reception room had been prepared for the

band, and Rosay had assured them it would be the talk of the evening. It was going to be a night to remember, that was for sure.

'Babes! Babes! Babes! It's all truly *Wonderbra*!'

Then, as they laughed, Barbie surprised them by giving them an envelope each.

'For you,' she said. 'You deserve it, girls. Even you, Rosay – I know you had your part in this and if your dad can pay you, then so can I! I don't mind answering to Carlo when I know I'm right.'

Amy peered inside hers and gasped. It was money – cash – and loads of it.

She thought of the huge bill she'd run up on her dad's credit card, and kept adding to, even after Rosay had handed over her share. This would cover it. Her worries would be over.

But still. It wouldn't be right.

'Oh, no, I can't accept this,' she told Barbie. 'I wanted to do this. And you've let me stay here! Honestly. It was no problem.'

Asha caught her eye and Amy could see what she was thinking. It was more than they could have earned in an entire summer at Water World. And Amy had lost them their jobs.

Amy went quiet. Maybe *she* didn't want to accept the money, but her friends should. And they had earned it, after all. Asha and Susi had worked as hard on this as she had.

But Susi spoke up. 'I'm with Amy. I did this as a favour, and to help my friend out. Thank you, Mrs di Rossi, but I'm giving this back.' She moved towards Barbie with the envelope held out.

'It's only what I was giving that useless party planner to start with!' Barbie said. 'Take it, really!'

Rosay waved her envelope around with a massive smile on her face. 'Well, Mum, I'm accepting mine.'

Barbie looked a bit disappointed, but she said, 'Course, babe, you earned it.'

'Although,' Rosay continued, 'I'm giving it to tonight's charity. Breast Cancer Aid, right, Amy?'

Amy nodded.

Asha gulped. Then she said, 'Me too! I'm doing what she's doing.'

Susi beamed at her sister. 'Brilliant idea! Can I do that too? It's a great cause.'

Amy blanked out all thoughts of the massive bill that would be arriving on her dad's doorstep. 'And me,' she said. 'Definitely. Thanks, everyone.'

'Aw, you lot! Suit yourselves!' Barbie gave a puzzled laugh that still somehow managed to shake white petals off a couple of the roses.

Rosay said, 'Sorry, guys but . . . Mum, can I speak to you alone for a minute?'

Amy and the twins went to finish getting ready, leaving Barbie shaking her head at her daughter and laughing to herself.

Later, as the reception rooms started to fill with people and chatter and clinking champagne flutes, Amy felt increasingly nervous. She moved to a corner of the room where she was relatively hidden and could spy on the arriving guests. She hadn't seen Damien for days. Would he talk to her? Would he arrive with Paige? Could she stand it?

Her thoughts were interrupted by a tall figure standing in front of her. It was Claudette, smiling in her trademark condescending way. She was wearing an amazing Roberto Cavalli turquoise dress and her neckline was awash with diamonds.

'Great party, darling,' she said.

'Thanks,' Amy muttered, feeling more like a sixteen-year-old than ever before.

'So. I'll get straight to business, so we can both relax and enjoy the night. Are you going to tell me what you know, or are you happy to be the talk of the tabloids next week?'

Amy swallowed hard. Rosay had told her things that Claudette would definitely want to know. She'd also made her promise not to tell anyone. 'I'm telling you because I trust you,' she'd said. 'Everyone else will find out pretty soon anyway, but you'll keep it quiet, won't you? I'll let everyone down if I spoil the surprise.'

And Amy had promised.

Claudette looked at her dainty gold watch. 'I'm waiting,' she said. 'I don't have all night.' She paused. 'Who is Miss X? What's all this stuff online and in the papers? These are things I know nothing about, that haven't been cleared with my PR guy, and that's not acceptable to me. I need to know, Amy.' She glared at her. 'And I know *you* know. Everyone knows you're Rosay's right-hand girl. So tell me.'

'It's . . .' Amy glanced around. She thought about Rosay, who wasn't perfect but at least had tried, in her own weird way, to be her friend. And Claudette, who was glaring at her right now, dying to cut her down to size.

'You'd better tell me quickly,' Claudette said. 'Your boy-friend's on his way over.'

Amy's heart leapt. Was Damien coming to speak to her? She glanced around, but she could only see crowds of familiar faces: models, actors, footballers, footballers' girlfriends, Boroughs staff.

'I don't know . . .' Amy muttered.

'You do know,' Claudette insisted. 'And your boyfriend's career is at stake.'

Amy squirmed, trying to think of a way to avoid Claudette's threats without betraying her friend.

'You have about ten seconds before he reaches us, and then your time's up. So tell me . . . who is Miss X?'

'It's . . .' It didn't feel right, telling Claudette when she'd promised not to. She felt bullied. Surely there was another way to work things out? Amy looked down, avoiding Claudette's eyes. 'I can't tell you. It's supposed to be a big surprise.'

Claudette scoffed. 'Suit yourself, baby. Well, here he is. I'll leave you to it.'

When Amy looked up, Claudette had gone and there, stand-ing in front of her, wearing a tux and looking utterly gorgeous was . . . not Damien.

It was Josh.

'Hi,' he said. 'What's up with Claudette? She left in a hurry.'

'Oh, nothing. Hi, Josh,' Amy said, trying to act natural. Also trying to hide her disappointment that he wasn't Damien. Did Claudette really think Josh was her boyfriend? What was that photo *like*?

'Are you OK?' he asked.

'Oh, great,' Amy joked half-heartedly. 'Are you analysing me already?'

Josh didn't laugh. 'I haven't seen you for days,' he said. 'You haven't been swimming.'

'Oh, I've been busy. Party planning and –' She didn't like to add 'shopping', although it was true.

'Well, you've done a great job.'

'Thanks. My friends did a lot, too. It was a bit daunting organizing something like this, but having an unlimited budget seemed to help.'

Josh nodded. 'I heard Barbie telling everyone she'd like to hire you for future events. She throws a lot of parties. It could be a full-time job.'

Amy smiled. 'Oh, no, I have to go back to Stanleydale after this. Back to the real world, you know.'

'Why? I know she meant it. You could be on the staff.' He looked deadly serious. 'Like me. My work placement's for a whole year.'

A waiter went past with a tray full of champagne cocktails.

'Meringue Royales,' Amy muttered, remembering the first party she'd gone to in London, at Scott White's house. Things had been so different then.

'You want one?' Josh asked.

'No – I –'

'I'll get you one.' Josh clicked his fingers and plucked a drink smoothly from the tray that wafted next to him as a result.

'Thanks,' Amy said to the waiter, who nodded and quickly dissolved back into the party's crowds.

'Here.' Josh handed the drink to Amy.

'Oh. OK. Thanks.'

Josh gave her a lovely smile as she sipped the drink she didn't want.

'So . . . I met your Stanleydale friend on the tennis court,' he said.

'Asha?'

'That's it. She's nice. She has a mean serve.'

Amy grinned. Asha had come back disappointed the other day, saying Josh was only interested in sport, but at least she'd used his spare racquet and very nearly trounced him even though she'd never played much tennis.

'Amy, can I say something?'

'Sure.' Was she imagining it or was he moving closer to her? She glanced around nervously. Not that she needed to worry about paps tonight – she'd hired the best security firm to police Caseydene, and she could see that the press people Claudette invited were busy with the charity reps. But still. What was he going to say? It looked important.

'It's just . . . I really think it would be fantastic if you considered Barbie's offer. I . . .' He glanced down. 'I don't want you to leave. I was wondering . . . If you don't go, or if there's time before you go . . .' He looked up, his eyes deep pools of blue. 'And I realize it's early days for you after your break-up.' He gave a nervous laugh. 'So no pressure, but . . . would you let me take you to dinner?'

Amy took a huge gulp of champagne and then choked, spluttering in a totally embarrassing way.

'Are you OK?' Josh asked. 'That's not me analysing you, I promise.' His tentative smile didn't reach his eyes. 'So . . .'

Amy coughed some more. 'Hold on.' Cough, cough. 'I'm fine. I –'

A huge crash from the other side of the room interrupted her, which Amy was secretly relieved about since she didn't have a clue what to tell the gorgeous guy who had just asked her out.

Because it made no sense, but Amy knew she didn't want to go out with him. She was attracted to Josh, but . . . he wasn't Damien.

Then she saw what had caused the crash. One of the buffet tables was on its side, the tablecloth stretched out, and food and crockery scattered all over the floor. And in the middle of the chaos was Poshie Pug himself. He was wearing a purple velvet bow around his neck that matched Kylie's classically styled Azzaro velvet dress.

Amy saw him eat several mouthfuls of extremely expensive canapés and then head for the next table, pulling at the dangling lace of the tablecloth.

'Poshie! Naughty boy!' Kylie's shrill voice sang out.

'Sorry, Josh. Excuse me.' Amy rushed over. She felt responsible for this party, and she felt an odd duty to save Barbie's luxurious flooring.

'Oh, Amy! Thank goodness! Help me catch him, would you?'

'Kylie.' Amy took a deep breath. 'Why have you brought your dog to the party?'

'Oh, I knew you wouldn't mind. I *had* to bring him – the Poshie-sitter called in sick! I don't know where Paige has got to – I need to look for her. She normally helps me keep an eye on him when we take him out to social occasions.'

Amy wondered how often that happened. She tried to push aside thoughts of where Paige could have got to, and whether she'd got there with Damien. She had a dog to catch, after all, and a buffet to save.

'Poshie! Omigod, don't eat that – it's a mini hot-dog! It's *inhumane*! That's, like, practically cannibalism!' Kylie reached frantically for her Pug, but overbalanced and collapsed into a tray of canapés, which exploded around her in a mess of flaky pastry and melted cheese. 'Omigod! My dress! Amy, stop him!'

Poshie must have sensed that his food supply was about to be cut off because he took one look at Amy and ran out of the room as fast as his little legs could carry him.

'Follow that dog!' Kylie yelled, getting up and teetering into the hallway in her sculpted heels, a canapé still stuck to her bum. 'Upstairs!'

Amy kicked off her Jimmy Choos and chased up the staircase way ahead of Kylie. Poshie sniffed at a few almost-closed doors and nudged his flat muzzle around one of them before disappearing inside the room. Amy noted with alarm that it was Rosay's dressing room. She'd been in there often enough to know that the room was a total mess of clothes, but somehow Rosay always seemed to know where everything was. She was sure to notice if Kylie's Pug rampaged through her stuff.

Amy pushed open the door, calling, 'Poshie, come here!'

She heard a yelping sound, too high-pitched and human to be Poshie. The same voice said, 'Poshie, did you sniff me out? I know you're happy to see me, but get off!'

It must be Rosay. She pushed open the door.

'Rosay, sorry but – oh.'

It wasn't Rosay.

It was Paige.

Paige Young was in Rosay's dressing room, sitting on the floor, with Poshie licking excitedly around her face and neck, pulling at her hair and jewellery.

Then a familiar figure came out of the en suite bathroom holding a fluted glass. He was tall and fit and dark and gorgeous and she'd recognize that walk anywhere.

Damien.

Paige was here with Damien.

Just when Amy thought things couldn't get any worse, Poshie leapt away from Paige and padded proudly up to Amy. Something glinted from his wrinkled muzzle – something that was caught there. Amy bent down and unhooked it.

It was a delicate chain with a heart pendant.

It was her necklace! The Tiffany necklace that Damien had given her when he'd moved to London, the one she'd lost in Caffe Americaine the day she'd seen Paige. The day Paige had looked guilty and pushed something into her pocket.

As if it wasn't bad enough that Damien had cheated on her with Paige.

As if it wasn't bad enough that she'd *caught* them together just now, in this room, this *bed*room, when they were supposed to be at the fundraising party *she'd* worked hard to arrange.

As if all that wasn't bad enough . . . it looked like Paige had been wearing *her* necklace, at least until Poshie attacked her.

And Damien must have known.

24

Damien froze. 'Amy!'

Paige groaned from where she was sitting on the floor. Then she said, 'Oh, wow, is that the necklace you lost before? The one Damien gave you?' Her voice was slurred, Amy noticed with disgust. So the rumours were true.

And here was Damien, plying her with more drink.

And Paige, pretending she hadn't stolen her necklace. And her boyfriend.

Amy could not believe what was going on.

Paige shuddered, then said in the same drunken voice, 'Oh, brilliant, did Poshie find it for you? Poshie, you're a star!'

Amy wasn't sure who to have a go at first, or what to shout. She'd never felt so angry in her life.

She took a deep breath and was about to lay into someone, anyone, and possibly the little Pug, too, when Kylie appeared, huffing in the doorway.

'Poshie! You naughty boy!'

'He's not naughty!' Paige slurred. 'He found Amy's necklace. Where was it, Poshie?'

Damien's deep voice rang out, surprising Amy. 'I saw him pull it out from over there, in that pile of Rosay's old clothes.'

Amy looked where he was pointing. She recognized some of the clothes from her first trip to Orange County, including one of the tops she'd tried on that day.

Could it be possible that the chain had got caught in the top and Rosay had taken it home by accident? Amy couldn't believe she'd forgotten all about that top. There had been so many clothes since then, so many shopping trips.

Kylie scooped up Poshie and knelt next to Paige, touching her forehead gently. 'Omigod, are you OK? Did you go hypo again?'

'I'm fine. Only two point eight.' Paige nodded at Damien. 'He noticed again.' It sounded like *notished*. 'He caught me before it was too late this time.' She smiled weakly at Amy, and Amy suddenly realized how pale Paige was looking, despite all her make-up. She was sweating and she looked droopy, like melting candle wax. She didn't look drunk, she looked . . . ill.

Paige's hands trembled as she waved them in Amy's direction. 'Don't tell anyone, OK, Amy? I didn't want you to know! I don't want *anyone* to know, but this lot bloody found out by mistake! It only started last year, and I hate any kind of sh-sh-special treatment.'

'Ssh,' Kylie soothed, but Paige shook her off.

Amy looked at Damien in confusion.

'She has diabetes,' he explained in a flat tone, barely meeting her eye.

'People feel sorry for me, and they say they understand, that it's easy to control nowadays.' Paige's face twisted with anger. 'But it's so not easy, living like this, not when you're *me*! And they *don't* understand! It's never-ending. I'll never get better – never, ever, ever! I'll never be normal! I can't even go on a

213

diet now! I can't always join in when everyone's drinking *champers*! I have to think about it all the time! If I don't, I end up in hospital and things could have been worse that night if it wasn't . . . if it wasn't for your boyfriend, Amy! And . . . and . . . no wonder Scotty doesn't love me any more!'

Kylie wrapped her arms around her. 'Ssh,' she said again. 'It's OK. Have you used your pump thingie?'

She lifted the side of Paige's top, revealing a gadget in her side, with a cord that led to a pocket in Paige's trousers. Kylie pulled out some kind of device.

Paige swatted Kylie away without much energy.

'Promise me you used it this time, or I'll force you to do it now,' Kylie said sternly.

Paige nodded weakly. 'Yesh. Damien made me use it. I wandered up here to lie down but the floor looked comfier. He was just getting me a glass . . . a glass of champers.'

Everyone looked at Damien in shock.

'It's water,' Damien said quickly. 'It's the only glass I could find in the bathroom.'

'Aw! I wanted champers. Or shum-thing.' Paige laughed. 'Not boring *water*.'

Damien frowned. 'It's for taking your glucose tablets.'

'They're chewable! Anyway, I don't need them. I'm feeling better. Is Scotty here? Have you seen him? Who's he with?'

Kylie winced. Then she looked up at Damien and Amy. 'Look, you two, thanks, but I think you should go. I'll stay with her.' She walked over and took Poshie from Amy's arms with one hand and the glass of water from Damien with the other. 'Leave Poshie with me, too. I can look after them both, honest, I'm not just an extremely pretty face!'

She smiled and batted her long lashes.

'Besides, it's my turn, Damien. You had that mega all-nighter the other night when I was at Johann's. I still feel bad about that.'

'It was no problem,' Damien said.

Paige moaned. 'I don't need looking after!'

'I'm not looking after *you*, silly.' Kylie nudged her friend, sitting next to her again and stroking her Pug's back. 'I'm looking after Poshie, and you're helping me. OK?'

She tickled the dog and Paige joined in half-heartedly.

'Good. Now. I'm glad I've got you here cos we can have a perfectly normal girlie gossip and no special treatment at all.' Kylie rested her head on Paige's shoulder. 'So, OK, let me tell you what's going to happen later, cos I got the inside scoop today. You will die when you hear this! For a start, me and Rosay are friends again – we had this long chat earlier, and you will not *believe* what she told me!'

'Come on, Ames, let's leave them to it,' Damien said softly, and, before Amy knew what was happening, he was cupping her elbow and steering her out of the room. She was so surprised at his touch, and at the way he'd said her name, that she let him lead her out of the room and down the corridor, down the stairs and on to the gravel of the Caseydene courtyard, where he leant against a tree.

He let go of her arm and looked at her in the damp summer moonlight. The muffled music and laughter from the party didn't fill the silence between them. He didn't smile.

Then he said, 'So. Are you going to stop the crazy jealousy now?'

'I didn't know,' Amy mumbled, still not quite sure she'd

understood. 'So Paige has diabetes? And she hides it from everyone, and she has funny turns?'

'Hypoglycaemia. It can lead to coma.' Damien's voice was hard. 'It's serious. A couple of times when I've been out with the lads, she's turned up and everyone has ignored her, or laughed at her, thinking she's drunk. But that Sunday after you first got here, when I saw her at the bar, I knew there was something wrong. I walked in on her using her insulin pump in a quiet corridor, and she told me about her diabetes but she made me promise not to mention it to anyone.' Damien sighed. 'Then the other night, when me and Scott got kept behind, she was waiting outside for him, sitting on the ground. And he just said hello to her and swanned off – he probably had a *date* or something.' Damien's face was screwed up in disgust. 'But I looked at Paige and I knew it was serious this time. I took her to hospital. I was scared, Amy. I wanted to phone you but it all happened so fast, and the hospital signs said to turn my phone off.'

Typical Damien, following the rules at all costs, Amy thought.

'Paige made me swear not to tell you, though I wasn't completely sure about that. But it was easy, because the next day you told me never to talk to you again.'

She bit her lip. 'So you were at the hospital that night? With Paige?'

'For a while. I couldn't get hold of Scott.' Damien said his name like it was dirt. 'How he can just go off like that while his girlfriend's ill? It's not right!' His eyes flared. 'Paige worries about her image, how the other girls see her, how Scott sees her. Between you and me, I don't think she's taking her insulin properly. She's trying to ignore it all – she seems to thinks her diabetes has put Scott off her. But really, he just doesn't care at all.' Damien shook his head. 'I thought he was a mate at first, but now I can't stand him, Ames.'

'Is that why you had that fight?'

Damien nodded grimly. 'It wasn't a fight. He was bragging about all these girls he was seeing, what he'd done on one of the nights when he left his girlfriend in the bar with us and went off. When she was obviously in trouble and needed him! And I . . . Well, we had words.'

Amy thought of Danny Harris. 'Fendi handbags at dawn?'

'Pardon?'

'Never mind. What happened at the hospital?'

'She told them I was her brother and I went along with it. Thankfully no one recognized me. They sorted her out and discharged her, so I took her home. Kylie was at Johann's, and I didn't have their numbers. Paige's family lives miles away and, to be honest, I'm not even sure she's told them. She's so used to being independent, even though she's only a bit younger than me. It's a funny world, this, Ames. You know that.'

Amy nodded. It really was. 'So you took Paige home and stayed with her?'

Damien nodded, his face earnest and sincere.

Then she realized something. She trusted Damien. It wasn't just because of what she'd found out about Paige's condition. She should have known he'd never cheat on her. She didn't know why she'd let her imagination run wild like that, even if Kylie's words had misled her. She knew what Damien felt for her! She knew what they had together, so why had she let herself think the worst, against her better judgement? Without even speaking to him. She'd got so carried away with what everyone thought of her, with living in the WAGs' world and fitting in with the others, that she'd stopped looking at what *she* really thought, what she really knew.

Damien gave her an imploring look. 'I slept on the sofa, Amy!'

'I know,' she said.

'I got covered in dog hair. But nothing happened apart from that! I can't believe you thought it did! Especially without even talking to me.'

'I know. Neither can I. When Kylie said you stayed over, I just lost it. I couldn't see any other possible explanation. I'm sorry.'

She moved closer to him and touched his arm, waiting for him to say 'I'm sorry too'.

But he shrugged her off and she thought her heart would break. For real this time.

'I don't know, Amy. It's not that simple.'

'Isn't it?' Amy shut her eyes. He wasn't going to take her back! He was angry. And he was right to be angry. She'd overreacted and, worst of all, she hadn't trusted him. He was going to break up with her now, properly, and she deserved this.

She heard his voice, each of his words laboured and concentrated, like he was finding them hard to pronounce.

'If you can't trust me . . . Well, maybe Josh was right. Maybe it's better if we make a clean break of –'

Amy opened her eyes. 'Hold on a sec. What did you say?'

'Maybe it's better if –'

'I mean, about Josh. What's he got to do with this?'

Damien stared at her. 'He said that now wasn't the right time for me to have a serious relationship, that my football would suffer. That it was better to be single at this stage in my career.'

'He said *what*?'

She was going to kill Josh. It was a familiar feeling. She'd felt like this before, back when Damien had suggested they needed space – and *that* had been Josh's fault too!

'But Damien, what if he's wrong? You can't just believe every word someone says. Not if it's about us, and you know better!' She'd just worked that out herself!

Damien frowned. 'But he's studied all this stuff, Amy. And he was hired by Big Carl himself. I have to do what's best for my career.'

'Yes, and also what's best for *us*!' Amy's mind raced. 'Damien, have you thought that it doesn't make sense? The only reason Big Carl let me come here is that this sports psychology guy told him personal relationships for players were important. Remember?'

'Yeah.'

'So why, when I get here, does the same guy suddenly tell you to distance yourself from me? And then to dump me?'

'I don't know. Because you've been acting jealous? Holding me back?'

'*How* have I held you back?'

Damien looked confused. 'I don't know.'

'That's because I haven't!' Amy sighed. 'Look, if we've had some fights, it's just because it's all a bit new and weird. For both of us. It's nothing a bit more time together wouldn't fix. Which is exactly the opposite of what Josh is telling you.'

'But why would he say that, then?'

'Because, maybe . . .'

Surely what Amy was thinking now couldn't be true? Could Josh have deliberately tried to break her and Damien up?

'Well, I think he kind of asked me out earlier on –'

'He did *what*?' Damien's eyes flared with anger. 'Are you going out with Josh?'

'Calm down! I didn't say yes.'

'Well, good!' He looked around wildly. 'Where is he? I'll kill him!'

'But Josh thought it was all over between us, didn't he?'

'Huh,' Damien muttered.

Amy nearly smiled at his reaction. Maybe there was hope for them after all. She decided it was probably better not to mention that Claudette had a photo where it looked like she and Josh were kissing. She'd tackle that some other time. Right now, all that mattered was her and Damien.

'You know, he probably didn't mean any harm, saying all those things – he just read our situation wrong.' Amy took a deep breath. 'But we're stronger than that. We can get through this, can't we?'

Damien shrugged stubbornly. 'I thought so before. But none of this changes the fact that you didn't trust me about the Paige thing.'

'Maybe I'd have trusted you more,' she said, 'if you'd told me what was really going on, and if you'd believed in *us* enough not to listen to some stranger about how much we should see each other.'

The beat of distant music pulsed in the air.

Damien gave a slow smile that made Amy's knees weak. 'You're right. I was wrong. I'm sorry.'

'I was wrong, too. I'm sorry, too.'

'Yeah, but I'm really sorry. I was really wrong.'

'I'm really sorry, too. I was really wrong, too.'

Damien reached over and took her hand. 'Yeah, but I was really, *really* wrong.'

And before she could say anything, he leant closer and kissed her softly once, twice.

It took her breath away.

He looked at her. 'I win.' He smiled.

She pushed him gently back against the tree. 'No, I win,' she said. Then she kissed him in the moonlight and didn't let him say anything else at all.

25

For a long time, Amy and Damien barely noticed the sounds that filled the night air, the soundtrack to their making up. A car pulled up outside Caseydene and loud laughter drifted across the courtyard, accompanied by the chatter of a crowd of people. A few minutes later there was a squeaky microphone announcement, first low pitched, then higher and longer. But it was the unexpected silence from the audience that made Amy pull away from Damien.

'I think the band are here,' she said. 'I promised I'd go and watch them. To support . . .'

Damien kissed her again and her mind went blank.

Soon she noticed there was definitely music playing, but something sounded unusual, for a live band. There was no whooping or cheering, no distant drunken voices trying to sing along.

'I really need to get in there, Damien. I promised Rosay.'

'I don't trust that girl,' Damien grumbled.

'She's been a good friend, honestly.'

'She's not a good person.'

'She's not all bad. I think a lot of people have been too hard on her.' Amy poked him gently in the ribs. 'Anyway, when I first got here, you told me Scott was a good person.'

'Ow. Point taken.' Damien sighed. 'I suppose we can give this band a listen, if you really want.'

'I do.'

She started to walk to the house, but he hesitated, his eyes dark. 'Can I talk to you later, though, Amy? About what we should do . . .' He cleared his throat. 'About us, I mean.'

Amy stared at him, but he wasn't looking at her. What did he mean? Amy had thought they were sorted now, back together, but it sounded like Damien wasn't so sure.

The music started up again. Amy didn't want to break her promise to Rosay.

'Yeah, OK. We'll talk later,' she said.

Damien took her hand as they made their way to the house, which confused her even more.

The buzz of low conversation as they walked in was more noticeable than the music. A few people were listening to the band, or dancing, but mostly people were in huddles, doing what Amy could only describe as gossiping. Especially the older people. There was a group of Barbie's friends with matching deep fake tans and gold high heels, all muttering things like 'Can't believe it!' and 'Shocking'. And she saw Big Carl stomping around, with Barbie patting his arm.

Dragging Damien with her, Amy got closer to the stage. There were four girls performing, and, just as Rosay had told her earlier, one of them was Rosay herself, dressed in a black sparkly cocktail dress and looking understatedly glamorous.

Amy smiled and waved and Rosay nodded at her but kept crooning into her microphone. Rosay told her she'd joined the group on Monday, after something Amy had said. She'd been rehearsing like mad with the others, but she'd also been well paid for agreeing to be in a new reality TV show.

Rosay hadn't told her who the other band members were; only that one of them would surprise everyone.

Amy recognized the backing singer next to Rosay from her first day in London – she was Courtney, the Boroughs goalie's girlfriend. Amy had never seen the girl next to Courtney before. But the lead singer – a tall, dark-skinned girl with long black hair streaked with extensions in five different shades of blonde – well, she looked very familiar, and it only took Amy another second to work out who she was.

The girls stopped singing their pop ballad and the streaky-haired singer shouted, 'It's great to be here at Caseydene for the start of the new season!'

No one cheered. A couple of people near Amy – a tall man and a woman with thick silver hair in a layered bob – clapped. Amy thought about joining in, but the applause ended quickly. It was beyond embarrassing and uncomfortable.

'I'm Trina Santos and our group is called The Miss Exes! Watch out for us on the newest reality show – *Bandwagon*! Yeah, we put the WAG in *Bandwagon*!'

Amy cringed to herself. Even Asha wouldn't come up with something as tacky as that. The gossiping instantly started up again. No wonder, Amy thought. Everyone must be connecting The Miss Exes to the Miss X in the gossip blog. And, earlier on, Rosay had finally told her that the Miss X scandals were partly a publicity stunt for the group and the new TV show. All four of the girls were Miss X, and they'd sold their stories at the same time, with the PR agency and *GossMonger.com* mixing things up a bit for maximum impact. Each band member had their own reasons for wanting to expose certain truths, though some of the reasons were more worthy than others.

Rosay hadn't said much about *Bandwagon*, though. Amy overheard the silver-haired woman next to her now, explaining the programme to her small audience of shocked-looking people. It was a reality show that would follow the progress of footballers' girlfriends in the music industry. It would feature an all-WAG girl band, facing off against Paige Young's 'rebranding as a solo artist'.

'A lot of it will be semi-live,' the woman added. 'We'll follow them to concerts, see who's the bigger draw, the band or the solo artist, and most of their profit will go to charity. Though I think they'll all make it big from this.'

'The public are bound to love this,' gushed one of the people the woman was talking to. 'You know how those gossip magazines sell. It sounds to me like cutting-edge television.'

Damien raised his eyebrows at Amy. 'It sounds to me like they're all going to murder each other,' he remarked quietly.

Trina was still yelling on stage. 'We're going to be *huge*. You heard it here first!'

The silver-haired woman applauded into the silence again. Amy looked around the room and noticed Claudette in a corner with Danny. Claudette's eyes caught hers and narrowed, and Amy quickly looked away, towards where Scott White was standing in the middle of a crowd of model-like girls. They all gazed adoringly up at him.

'This next one is called "You're a Creep". It's adapted from a classic Radiohead song and it's dedicated to our favourite Boroughs striker.' Trina shook her amazing mane of hair.

Amy saw Claudette nudge Danny, who held out his palms in a gesture that said 'It wasn't me, ref!'

Trina shouted, 'Scott White, this one's for you! *You're a Creep!*'

Then someone cheered loudly.

Everyone's eyes turned in the direction of the sound.

Kylie was standing by the doorway with Poshie in her arms. When she saw everyone look at her, she widened her eyes and said, 'What? I've always liked that song.'

The silver-haired woman whispered to the people near her, 'That's my niece.'

So she was Kylie's auntie Fran, who was something important in television! Amy should have realized. In that case, the person who'd done Kylie a huge favour by letting her drop out of the band was Rosay. No wonder Kylie and Rosay were speaking again.

Big Carl stomped about, grumbling. 'You see? Wives and girlfriends are a problem! I don't care what the psychologists say! I'm going to take the boys away for training, to some faraway place with no disruptions!'

Barbie ignored him. 'That's my baby up there! She has the voice of an angel! I'm so proud!'

The music started up, a slow, thumping beat, and Trina began singing the song, though it sounded more like howling. Kylie danced and a couple of people joined her, and some even sang along to the tuneless lyrics.

This time, when the song was finished, there was a loud burst of applause from the girls that had been worshipping

Scott White, and it rippled around the room until nearly everyone was clapping. But Amy couldn't see any sign of the infamous striker himself. He must have left somewhere in the middle of the song.

Trina shouted, 'We're going to take a break now but we'll be back in a few minutes! Ladies, gentlemen . . . and foot-ballers.' Her voice became a roar: 'We are The Miss Exes! You saw us here first!'

Damien squeezed Amy's hand.

'Want a drink?' he asked her. 'One of those cocktail thingies?'

'Orange juice, please,' she said. Meringue Royales weren't really her style. She'd had enough of trying to fit in.

Instead of clicking his fingers in a Josh-like way, Damien spotted a waiter in the distance. 'OK. I'll be right back.'

Amy watched her gorgeous boyfriend disappear into the crowd.

Or was he still her *ex*-boyfriend?

She thought about everything that had happened between her and Damien since she'd got here. Well, one thing was for sure: whatever he wanted to speak to her about later, she wasn't going to give up on this relationship without a fight.

She opened her clutch bag, where she'd put the Tiffany necklace after Poshie had found it. She couldn't wait to tell Rosay where it had been. She reached behind her neck to put it on.

She was just doing up the clasp when Claudette appeared in front of her again. And she didn't look happy.

'So, baby. Back with your ex, I see?'

'I hope so.'

'You hope so?'

Why should she be honest with Claudette? 'No, I mean, I am.'

It was hard not to feel nervous, but Amy thought she could manage it. After all, she knew how to play the game. The secret was to believe in what you knew was true. You couldn't let anyone put doubts in your mind. She'd come a long way since her arrival in London two weeks ago. She knew how to handle herself now.

'Well, darling,' Claudette drawled. 'Game's over, and you've lost. You didn't tell me about the Trina Santos comeback, you didn't tell me about Rosay, you didn't tell me any of this. I would have particularly appreciated a warning about Trina's big announcement.'

Amy frowned. 'Er, what announcement?'

'Oh, wait, of course.' Claudette said. 'You were outside when they first came on. Well, you missed a treat. Apparently Trina's a changed person after her time abroad caring for sick orphans.'

Amy was confused. Rosay hadn't mentioned anything about Trina, including this. 'I thought she was a model in Brazil?'

'She did the orphan thing in her spare time.' Claudette snorted in a way that vaguely reminded Amy of Poshie. 'So she's a born-again truth-teller now. She's all about the public confessions.'

'Confessions?'

'Yes, darling. As you must have known, but chose not to warn me about, she came on and confessed to the whole room that she was guilty of trashing Paige's clothes last year, after all.'

Amy couldn't believe what she was hearing. 'Are you saying Trina slashed Paige's clothes? Not Rosay?'

'That's right. Poor Rosay, taking the rap all that time, at least among her friends and family. She's so saintly.' Claudette gave a sickly smile. 'It's a shame even her own family were so sure she was guilty.'

'I bet her mother wasn't.' She wondered if Barbie suspected the truth, but she got swept along in what everyone else thought. The same as Amy had been doing lately.

Claudette's smile didn't waver. 'Anyway, Trina isn't that much of a saint with her confessions. She only told half the story. She still knows what's good for her.'

'What do you mean?'

'Amy, baby, I wasn't kidding when I say that I control the wives and girlfriends. As I've already told you, it's *us* who run the team. And *I* run *us*. So it all comes down to me. I control the Boroughs. I decide who's in, and who's out.'

Claudette shook her jewellery.

'I can play the game better than anyone, and I *always* win. Look at last year. Paige, Rosay, Trina, they all suffered. But there were two of us at the flat that day. And I'm absolutely fine!'

Amy frowned. 'Wait. Are you saying you were with Trina when she did that thing to Paige's stuff?'

'*With* her, darling? I put the idea in Trina's head! Paige needed to be put in her place. She stole my hairdresser! Rico's good, but Patrice was better. And anyway, Paige made no effort to fit in with the team. I was sick of that baby acting like she was better than me.'

Amy felt totally shocked. 'So *you* trashed Paige's clothes?'

Claudette looked horrified. 'Oh, no, I wouldn't stoop that low. Trina did it – I just had to work her up a bit, talk up the Scott betrayal, back-date it a little to make it look like it happened before Trina and Scott were breaking up anyway. And then I was kind enough to cover Trina's tracks. I do that kind of thing brilliantly.'

Claudette gave Amy a serious look. 'I hope you can see now *why* I'm telling you this. What I'm showing you, Amy, is that I'm the kind of person you want as a friend, not as an enemy.'

Amy stared at her. She couldn't believe she was really hearing this.

'You were wrong not to tell me about tonight's gossip. But I'm very generous.' Claudette jangled her earrings. 'Now that Rosay won't play any more, I need a replacement. So I'm prepared to let you off ... if you'll take over from Rosay. Keep your ear to the ground for me, get the gossip, you know the kind of thing. It'll be easy. You can get the best stuff from Rosay herself. She thinks you're great – the word she used was "genuine". She won't suspect a thing.'

Amy stared at Claudette in disbelief.

'So what do you say, baby? When can you start?'

Amy forced herself to meet Claudette's eyes. 'Never. I'm not doing it.'

Claudette narrowed her eyes. 'I don't believe you, darling. Gossip can be so damaging. Don't you want to work for the good of my team?'

Amy took a deep breath. 'Claudette, it's not *your* team. It's everyone's team. It's *our* team. And I don't think you care about the gossip at all. I think what you're worried about is losing control. You're worried you won't be the one everyone looks to any more. You're scared of Rosay – and Trina Santos – getting one over on you. That's what this is about.' She hesitated. 'And I don't want to be a part of it.'

Amy couldn't believe she'd said all that to Claudette! Had she gone too far?

But she knew she was right. And if there was one thing she'd learnt in the past couple of weeks, it was that you had to stand up for the truth.

'Oh, Amy, look at you! You're finally all grown up!' Claudette shook her head. 'Wait, though. How sweet! You're *analysing* me! Did you get that from your psychologist boy-friend? He's left the party, you know. I think it was after he saw your little display outside.'

'What?'

'We *all* saw it, darling! Well, everyone who was standing near the doors. Barbie called us into the courtyard to welcome the arrival of the band, and there you were, all over your ex!'

Amy cringed at the thought that she and Damien had had an audience.

'You're such a heartbreaker, Amy Thornton! Poor Josh, and poor Damien.' She pursed her lips. 'What *will* Damien say when that photo gets out? And I can definitely make it sound like you cheated on him before you two had your squabble. I'm sure the people of your cute hometown, including your parents, will be very proud of you.'

'Fine,' Amy said through gritted teeth. 'I can deal with it.'

'Deal with what?' Damien appeared with the drinks. 'Hi, Claudette.'

'Hi, my darling. I was having a pleasant chat with your little *ex*-girlfriend.' She scowled at Amy and walked away.

'What was all that about?' Damien asked, holding out a tall glass of orange juice.

'Oh, nothing. Just sport.' Amy took the drink and sipped it, thinking. If Damien saw that picture, could she make him understand? Maybe not, judging by the way he'd been so furious about Josh asking her out. Well, she didn't want to think about it right now.

'I've been talking to the twins.' Damien made an exhausted face. 'They seem to have spotted that we're talking again. Asha said she'd get the full explanation from you later, but she gave me a hard time anyway.'

'Sounds like Asha.'

'Susi was really off with me but she said if you were happy, she was happy.'

'Sounds like Susi.' Amy thought about how much she loved her friends. 'I should go and speak to them – I've barely seen them all night.' She tugged at his sleeve. 'You coming? You can help me convince them that you're not evil after all.'

He took her hand but didn't move. 'They said you were going back home with them tomorrow. Is that true?'

Amy looked down at her hand, clasped in Damien's. 'I don't know.' She took a swig of orange juice.

But she'd decided not to play games with Damien. She wanted him to know how she really felt. She needed to make it clear that she would fight for their relationship.

'No, I *do* know.' She looked deep into his eyes. 'I want to stay. With you. I want to move back to the cottage.'

There. She'd said it.

But when Damien didn't respond, she added nervously, 'Just for a bit longer.'

There was a long silence while Damien stared at the ground.

'I don't know about that,' he said, finally.

She took another massive gulp of orange juice and tried hard not to sound desperate. 'Damien, I know we've just had a bad . . .' Argument? Break-up? Neither seemed right. 'But I really . . . Don't you think we . . .'

'Amy. Shush. After I spoke to the twins I saw Kylie. She said Paige is sleeping now, in Rosay's dressing room. Good thing Paige missed the "Scott White Is a Creep" song.'

Amy tried to smile. 'She might have enjoyed it.'

'I don't think so. She's in pieces about the whole thing.'

'Oh.' Amy reminded herself not to feel jealous about Damien knowing Paige so well. He was allowed to have female friends. It hadn't mattered in the past and it didn't matter now. 'Poor Paige. Listen, I want you to know that I understand if you want to go and see her and stuff and I won't –'

'Amy. Shush.' He reached over and ran her Tiffany heart pendant through his fingers. 'I want to ask you something.'

'What?'

He let go of her necklace and his fingers brushed her neck. She trembled at the sensation.

'Kylie's been wanting to move out for ages. She's all set to move in with Johann but she's worried about leaving Paige. So I said . . .'

He looked straight into her eyes, his Adam's apple bobbing as if he was nervous. But why would he be nervous?

'I said we – you and me – might be able to move in with

233

Paige, into Kylie's room, and there's the dog's room too, of course. Kylie's taking Poshie to Johann's. There's loads of space at Spooky Towers and the rent's paid until the end of the month. And I thought it would do you good – do *us* good – to get away from Caseydene and be together, away from here, I mean, and –'

'Damien,' Amy said. '*You* shush.' She took his other hand. 'That's a brilliant idea. If Paige doesn't mind, I'd love to. Well, on two conditions.'

He interlocked his fingers with hers. 'Anything. What?'

'Well, the first one is that you invite me on your nights out sometimes.'

He squeezed her hand. 'OK. I'd like that, Ames.'

'And the other one is that we spend the whole of your next day off together. My treat. I want to take you out for chips.' She held her breath, wondering whether he would accuse her of not taking his diet seriously, or say that Big Carl needed him somewhere else and she wasn't putting his career first.

But his eyes lit up. 'With curry sauce?'

'I'm sure we can find some around here somewhere.'

'You're the best girlfriend any lad could hope for!'

And she pulled him close and kissed him, right in front of a whole roomful of glamorous people she wasn't scared of any more.

Will Amy's indulgent shopping sprees come back to haunt her?
And what will happen when she falls into a trap of blackmail and scandal?

Find out in the second book in this wildly addictive new series . . .